CU00956326

OPERATION
OSKAR

01962 826100

ALSO BY MAX HERTZBERG

The East Berlin Series
Stealing The Future (2015)
Thoughts Are Free (2016)
Spectre At The Feast (2017)

Reim Series
Stasi Vice (2018)
Operation Oskar (2019)
Berlin Centre (2019)

Other Fiction
Cold Island: A Brexit Novel (2018)

Non-fiction
with Seeds For Change
How To Set Up A Workers' Co-op (2012)
A Consensus Handbook (2013)

After the experience of the East German political upheaval in 1989/90 Max Hertzberg became a Stasi files researcher. Since then he has also been a book seller and a social change trainer and facilitator.

Visit the author's website for background information on the GDR, and guides to walking tours around the East Berlin in which many of his books are set.

www.maxhertzberg.co.uk

OPERATION OSKAR

MAX HERTZBERG

P 1 2 3 4 5 6 7 8 9 10

Published in 2019 by Max Hertzberg
www.maxhertzberg.co.uk

Copyright ©Max Hertzberg 2019.

Max Hertzberg has asserted his right under the Copyright, Designs
and Patents Act 1988 to be identified as the author of this work.

Cover photograph copyright ©Ungry Young Man, licensed under the
Creative Commons Attribution 2.0 International Licence.

Text licensed under the Creative Commons Attribution-Non-
Commercial-No-Derivatives 4.0 International License. View a copy
of this license at: www.creativecommons.org/licenses/by-nc-nd/4.0/

c/o Wolf Press, 22 Hartley Crescent, LS6 2LL

A CIP record for this title is available from the British Library
ISBN: 9781913125004 (paperback), 9781913125011(epub)

Set in 10½ on 12pt Linux Libertine O

All characters in this publication, except for those named public figures who
are used in fictional situations, are fictitious and any resemblance to real
persons, living or dead, is entirely unintended and coincidental.

This book is sold subject to the condition that it shall not, by way of trade or
otherwise, be lent, resold, hired out, or otherwise circulated without the
publisher's prior consent in any form of binding or cover other than that in
which it is published and without a similar condition, including this condition,
being imposed on any subsequent purchaser.

SEPTEMBER 1983

1
BERLIN
HOHENSCHÖNHAUSEN

"Where were you between 1600 and 2200 hours on the night of the fifteenth?

My comrades love a good question, maybe that's why they were asking me again. And again.

And again.

OK, I know what you're thinking. Why didn't I just answer?

But I'd already answered. I'd given them my answer this morning. And yesterday. And the day before.

And guess what? They were still keen to hear what I had to say.

I knew the procedure, I knew what to expect—I'd been on the other side of that table many times. I'd heard the lectures at the Ministry school in Golm and I'd read the manual. But this time I was in the hot seat. Knees closed tighter than a nun's, hands pressed under my thighs, palms pushed against the seat. No sleep for two days. Or was it three? Couldn't really tell whether the hallucinations were from alcohol withdrawal or lack of sleep.

Probably both.

So I gave them my answer again: "I was in my office, opening a preliminary file on a potential informant in Potsdam. The gate records will confirm that I spent the whole night at the headquarters of Main Department VI in Treptow."

The Stasi major sitting behind the desk didn't react. Didn't even bother looking up from the sheet of questions in front of him, just read out the next one from his list.

I didn't need a sheet of paper in front of me, I knew which question was next because he'd already asked me, as had the interrogator before him, and the one before that.

Like I said, they love a good question.

The shifts changed. The faces opposite me changed. But I stayed right where I was, and that list of questions stayed right there on the desk.

Every day or so they let me go back to shiver in my cell, just for a bit of variety. My cramped legs struggled to carry me down the cold corridors, my hands were shackled together and my head was lowered.

I couldn't see much. The traffic light system was above my line of sight, my vision topped out at the thin wires strung along the walls at shoulder height.

I thought about reaching out, pulling the fine wire before my guard could react. Break the electrical connection and the alarm would go off, more screws would turn up, truncheons ready for action. Surely the pain and the bruises would be better than this monotony?

Just for a bit of variety.

They were having a hard time deciding whether my dead Boss was a hero or a traitor and they expected me to help them work it all out.

Everyone else who could help was either dead or in the West. Either way, they were out of reach.

Fair enough, it was going to take them a bit of time to figure it out: all they had was the Boss's corpse with a big hole in the chest where a bullet had been dug out of it. They didn't know who had killed him.

But that wasn't the important bit.

They wanted the *why*. If they knew why he'd been killed they'd know whether he was a class-hero or a class-traitor.

Once the brass agreed on the why they might declare him a hero—just for the propaganda value—even if they'd decided he was a traitor.

Or it might happen the other way round. Who could say how it might turn out?

And me? I couldn't care less whether my dead Boss was a hero or a traitor. I only cared what the comrades thought. The interrogation notes would be sent to Berlin Centre, and one day the verdict would come back.

If the bigwigs decided the Boss was one of the bad guys then I was as good as dead.

2
BERLIN
HOHENSCHÖNHAUSEN

They returned my clothes and put me in the back of a Barkas van, a hard hand shoved me into one of the narrow cells. The door slammed before I could even turn around.

My shoulder hit the wall as we accelerated away. My hands were still cuffed in front of me and I dug my elbows into the scratched and pockmarked sides of the cell—my only chance of staying upright as the van twisted through corners.

There was nothing for me to do but count stops and turns. After a long run down a stretch of straight road, halting briefly for traffic lights, I felt the van pull off to the side. Cobbles rumbled under the wheels and the brakes squealed like a tram going around a tight curve.

When the cell door opened, a *Feldwebel* undid my shackles and stood aside to let me out.

I was nauseous with fatigue and disorientation, but made it out of the Barkas and took a first look at the world outside the prison walls. I knew this place, I knew the broken steps that led up the steep bank of trees.

Those steps were good news. Those steps were the side entrance to Volkspark Prenzlauer Berg. Slap bang in the middle of Berlin.

If you're going to shoot someone in the back of the neck, you don't do it in the middle of the city.

★

Behind me, life went on as normal. The traffic on Hohenschönhauser Strasse hummed like a beehive worried about a visit by a bear and his paw.

I didn't turn around when I heard the Barkas' two-stroke engine wind itself up to join the traffic flow, and I didn't turn around when the little engine faded into the background buzz of the traffic.

Like some eco-freak, I kept my eyes on the trees in front of me. Bright leaves floated down, flirting with the breeze that stroked my hair, gentler than any paid lover.

Sometime, while I was in that cell, autumn had arrived. You could tell by the yellow of the poplar and the bronze of the oak—not something I'd bother noticing under normal circumstances.

The sound of a familiar voice made me turn around.

"Comrade Lieutenant Reim?" It was an *Uffzi* from the Clubhouse. He had his heels pressed together, his forefinger stuck to his forehead and the rear door of a Chaika open.

I didn't bother with questions, there had been enough of those lately. I just climbed into the limo and the staff sergeant closed the door and ran around to the driver's side.

He took me home.

He took me the long way round, past S-Bahn station Leninallee. And that suited me just fine—I wasn't in the mood to wave to the Comrade Minister at Berlin Centre.

I had one hand balled up in my lap, trying to hide the shivers, the other held the curtains back. I watched Berlin pass by on the other side of the murky windows and imagined the taste of my next drink.

When I got to my flat, I went straight to the kitchen and poured myself a vodka.

I necked it. Then another.

Feeling more human, I stripped off my grimy clothes and stood naked in the kitchen, readying myself for another hit from the bottle. Only then did I go to stand under the shower.

I stayed there until I could no longer see the grime thread towards the plughole, and then I stayed for a bit longer.

Freshly washed and shaved, I went back to the kitchen and re-introduced myself to the bottle. There were no objections when I suggested we should go to bed together.

3
BERLIN FRIEDRICHSHAIN

The Chaika was outside my flat the next morning. I made the *Unteroffizier* wait while I dragged a blade over my chin and a brush over my teeth. Then I made him wait again at the first kiosk we passed.

I got out of the car and fetched myself a deck of cigarettes to cane and a fresh bottle of vodka to woo.

When we got to the clubhouse, the *Uffzi* stood guard outside my office as I changed into my service uniform, and then he marched me upstairs to the office that had once belonged to my Boss.

A captain was sitting behind the desk, and he looked all wrong. The Boss had been broad and tall, his shaven skull reflected the ceiling light and his presence filled the room. This officer looked more like the water tower at Ostkreuz station: lanky with a full helmet of dark hair.

His fine fingers were playing with a metal *Markant* fountain pen while his eyes pretended to scan the folder lying on the desk in front of him.

The *Uffzi* did the whole clicky-heels trick while I just stood to attention, waiting to hear my fate.

"Comrade Second Lieutenant Reim," Lanky began. He paused to lay his pen on the desk, diligently lining it up so it was parallel with the edges. Then he got round to looking at me. There was no polite chit-chat, no how-do-you-dos.

I faced forward, glaring at the wall above the captain's head while he gave me the up and down. He grew bored of it after a bit and started to talk:

"The investigation into the death of Major Fröhlich is ongoing. You are not to approach any person involved in or subject to the investigation."

"*Jawohl*, Comrade Captain!"

"We wouldn't want you to end up in Hohenschönhausen prison again."

"*Jawohl*, Comrade Captain!" I repeated. They like that kind of thing.

Satisfied, the captain dismissed me. I about-turned and followed the *Uffzi* out. We went into the secretary's office next door, and my guard dog did the announcements.

The secretary looked at me through her pink-framed glasses as if she'd never seen me before, then handed over a file. "The comrade captain requests that the Operational Process begins with immediate effect."

"Does the comrade captain have a name?" That earned me another stare through the pink glasses.

She delved deep, searching for a reason not to tell me but came up empty. "Captain Funke," she conceded.

I took the folder and went back to my office, ignoring the NCO as he clicked his heels and goose-stepped off.

The folder was the usual shape and size, the usual buff colour, identified only by the usual jumble of letters, numbers and coloured stripes on the front.

I sat at my desk and looked at the cover for a while then fetched a glass from the bottom drawer of the filing cabinet and looked at that instead. I lit a cigarette and filled the glass from the bottle I'd bought this morning, then toasted the room at large.

"Here's to good fortune," I told the walls, wondering why I was in such an optimistic mood.

4
BERLIN TREPTOW

Magpie was the perfect operation for a goon entertaining the thought that he might be off the hook and back in the Firm's good books. Couldn't have come up with anything more symbolic myself.

Twenty kilometres south of Schönefeld airport there's a landfill site. In return for hard currency, the Party takes West Berlin's trash off their hands, no questions asked. Capitalist bin lorries enter the GDR via their own checkpoint, trundle down the F96 like a line of ants on their way to a crumby party and dump their cargo on the edge of a nature conservation area.

From my comfortable chair in the Clubhouse, that was all fine by me. But I could tell from the first few pages that the file was winding itself up to the usual political-operational recommendations.

Typical of the Firm, trust no-one and trust the *Westler* even less. But trust our own people least of all, particularly if they're anywhere near said Westerners.

I took another shot of vodka and flipped to the end of the file to get a slant on the operational plan. And there it was: *member of the operative personnel to be engaged in conspirational activities as manual labourer at the site.*

The bastards were going to send me to snoop on workers at a rubbish dump.

5
SCHÖNEICHE

The Brigade Leader handed me a bucket full of plastic bags and a trowel.

"Take a sample from each lorry's load, seal the bag. Bring them back when your bucket's full."

I took the bucket but didn't give an answer. The Brigade Leader was short and stout, had hair on the back of his hands and fingers, but none up top. He wasn't the kind to need answers.

"And no talking to the *Westlers*!" he shouted after me.

I hiked along the track, rough chunks of construction waste held together by mud. Orange lorries from the West Berlin municipal waste company churned along, kicking up brown water and grey sludge as they passed.

By the time I'd reached the sector where the refuse was being poured out of the back of trailers, I was considering how to cut drainage holes in my boots.

When the next tipper starting lowering its trailer, I scooped up some crud—looked like coffee grounds mixed with potato peelings and rotten fruit—and emptied it into a bag. What's to report? I did that for the next hour, shovelling the shit the Westerners no longer wanted—nappies, building rubble, slow liquid that steamed in the cold air.

When my bucket was full, I trekked back to the machinery park near the gatehouse.

The foreman got out of an armchair that looked like it had been rescued off the back of a lorry and shuffled over to me.

He eyed my bucket in surprise and pointed towards a galvanised bin.

"You're keen!" he shouted as I tipped the contents of my bucket onto a bed of plastic bags, all filled with the slough of capitalism. On the way out I picked up another bucket.

The Brigade Leader was still shaking his head as I left.

For my next bag I selected a disposable nappy—it stank worse than Leuna on a still day. When I straightened myself after finishing the task, an orange-clad truck driver had set himself up by my side and was offering a Marlboro.

I took the cigarette and held it to my nose.

It smelt different, smoother than the coffin nails I'm used to. Even the truck driver smelt different from the workers I was used to—his musky deodorant was almost strong enough to cover the *eau d'ordurs* that surrounded us.

"Not seen you before?" The West Berliner said.

I took a light and looked him over. His overalls were smeared with grease. His sideburns hung below his cheeks, his chin hung over a blue work-shirt and his beer belly hung over his belt.

He shoved the lighter back into a pocket on the chest of his overalls, and it made a bulge between the S and the R of the company logo stamped there.

"First day," I told him as he handed me the packet of cigarettes.

"Keep 'em—we get them cheap from the duty-free shop at the entrance," he confided, adding his Western cigarette ash to all the other Western waste we were standing on. "Anything you need?" he asked, cocking an eyebrow at me.

The next truck had arrived and I moved into its slipstream, plastic baggie at the ready.

"Just give me a shout, you think of anything you want from over there," he nodded northwards, towards Berlin. "Ask for Detlef."

As he drove off I memorised the number plate of his tractor unit.

The other truck drivers that day didn't have much to say. Some nodded, others ignored me. But, on the whole, I was offered more cigarettes than I could smoke.

Just before the end of my shift, I took my two buckets back to the garage. The Brigade Leader was still in his armchair. He had his mouth full and his evening snap splayed open on his lap—buttered grey bread with sliced sausage and onion on top.

"Chuck them in the bin with the others," he said, spitting crumbs.

I emptied the buckets into the metal bin and left the foreman to his sandwiches.

At the gate, I watched the last of the West Berlin trucks jack-knife through the entrance and accelerate down the rough lane. There was no sign of any transport for workers, I'd have to walk back to my billet in the next village.

The Firm had sorted me out with lodgings in Gallun, a room in a widow's house. I'd arrived this morning, and before I left for the late shift the landlady had already asked me to make sure to keep my things tidy.

I looked around the room—the bed was made, all my things were still in a suitcase. The only thing she could have been referring to was the half-full ashtray next to the half-empty bottle of *Doppelkorn* on the night stand.

The landlady may be a dragon, but the house was on the edge of the village and my room had a dormer window overlooking the entrance to the landfill—just over a kilometre as the bullet flies.

I sat there drinking beer and watching the floodlit gates. Every so often a patrol would wander around the buildings before returning to the gatehouse. I opened another bottle.

6
SCHÖNEICHE

The next day, when I clocked on for the late shift, the Brigade Leader gave me a single rubber glove, long enough to reach my elbow.

I trudged up the rubble road as orange lorries went by on the way to dump their household waste. A white tipper truck, smeared with mud and grease, growled along behind before overtaking. West German plates.

When I got to where it was unloading I could see liquid waste spewing out of the raised tailgate, trickling over the ground and into the crevasses and voids in the rubbish that was already there.

I stood by, waiting for the West German to finish. The glove was more holes than rubber, and the lorry driver watched impassively as I tried to avoid contact with the stinking liquid while spooning a sample into a bag.

The driver shook his head and climbed back into his cab, moving the vehicle forward as he lowered the bed, leaving an oily pool in his wake.

As the lorry drove off, I spooned another glob of the viscous green liquid into a glass jar and screwed the lid on. It glimmered in the grey sunlight as I wrote the lorry's registration number and the date and time on the label.

I didn't write any information on the plastic bags, the gaffer hadn't told me to.

★

By the time the next lorry arrived, the sun had given up. The sky was blanketed with clouds the same grey as the waste ground, and a fine rain was destabilising the mud beneath my feet. The lorry slithered to a halt in front of me and reversed to the unloading point. Sludge skeetered over the tail as the bed was jacked up. The lorry moved forward and I took a sample of oil-saturated sawdust and tied the bag.

"Looks like you could use these," said the driver. He was standing next to me, holding out a pair of chemical gloves.

I looked at the frayed glove on my right hand, then at the Western ones the driver was offering.

Maybe I should have refused the offer—the driver was a lackey of the class-enemy—but I took the gloves and offered him a cigarette in return.

He laughed at my rain-sodden deck of coffin nails and opened up a fresh pack of Lucky Strikes. He took one for himself and gave me the rest.

"From the Intershop?" I asked.

"Yeah, the duty-free next to the entrance." The driver inhaled and poked the mound of toxic waste with the toe of his boot. "Some of the lads stock up, take a few cartons home, sell them in the pub."

I nodded politely and tried my new gloves for size.

"Right, got to get going—long haul ahead." The driver flicked his cigarette butt into a puddle and went back to his cab. He climbed in, then leant out of his window and shouted back to me, "Do you want a lift down to the gate?"

The rain was persistent now, the dirt beneath my feet was soft and growing softer and slippier. I thought of the gaffer in his armchair in the garage and shook my head.

"Suit yourself," the West Berliner drove off, his wheels spitting up mud and worse.

As soon as the lorry had crested the next ridge, I set out after it, taking short steps and firmly planting each foot before planning my next move.

I had to be quick about it though, each time I put a foot down, it began to sink into the slurry.

Twenty minutes later, I'd made it to the garage. The Brigade Leader was throwing plywood and bits of old window frame into a brazier and other workers were also there, crowding around the fire.

The conversation dulled into silence when they saw me, but I was handed a bottle of schnapps and I took a pull. The alcohol heated me from inside. I held my hands out, letting the flames warm them from the outside, all the while ducking out of the way of smoke whipped by draughts coming through the open front.

An older fellow was next to me, his moustache streaked with grey, the backs of his hands puckered with age. To my right was a milk-face, barely out of school. He was trying to grow a moustache but the blonde fuzz was still shy.

The bottle did the rounds again and I took another mouthful, then lit up one of my Lucky Strikes. Nearly everyone was smoking and from what I could see and smell, they were all pulling on Western Brands.

Conversation had started up again on the other side of the circle, but the colleagues near me remained silent.

The hissing of hydraulics made me turn to the entrance. One of the orange trucks from West Berlin had drawn up outside. Detlef climbed down from the cab and came over to the brazier, accepting the bottle of schnapps on the way.

He did the rounds, starting with the gaffer, shaking each man's hand in turn. "The new guy," he said when he got to me. "Hope they're not working you too hard?" He didn't wait for an answer, was already greeting the veteran next to me.

When he got to milk-face, the pair of them went back to the lorry. The East German waited at the edge of the garage while Detlef climbed the steps to the cab and pulled out a long cardboard box covered in a jacket. He dragged the jacket aside and handed the plain box into the worker's hands.

They came back into the garage, the box was put on a chair and opened up.

"That what you wanted, Erich? Is that the goods?"

Erich pulled out a white portable radio-cassette player, turning it over in his hands, eyes wide with wonder. He traced the brand name, *Sharp*, with a quivering finger, his eyes caressed the many buttons and switches and scanned the English labels. Plugging it in, Erich extended the aerial and nudged the dial until he found a clear signal.

The guitar solo from *Moonlight Shadow* zipped through the garage while Erich gawped at the radio. A sugary jingle intruded on the end of the song and Erich quickly pulled the plug when he realised we were listening to the West Berlin broadcaster SFB.

While this was happening, the rest of the workers remained at the brazier. Apart from me and Detlef, no-one was paying any attention to Erich and his radio.

"How much do you want for it?" asked Erich.

"Five," replied Detlef, holding his hand out.

Erich pulled five notes out of his pocket. The blue ones, one hundred West German Marks each. Take black-market exchange rates into account and five hundred Westmarks would be the equivalent of about six month's wages for young Erich.

Detlef rubbed the notes between his thumb and forefinger before putting them away, then he turned to me. "What about you, new boy? You in the market?"

"Nothing I need," I told him.

"Get you a nice portable stereo like that one. Or something second hand, if you want to pay less."

"That be something you've pulled out of the bin?"

"Suit yourself." Detlef was already at his truck, but with a few quick strides I caught up with him.

"My girlfriend was asking about a decent radio-cassette," I said.

"Got a girl, have you? So tell me, new boy, how much is this girl worth?"

I shrugged. Behind me, the workers around the brazier were looking my way.

"I can get you something new, like Erich's. Or something bigger, bit more oomph? Or, if you like, I can keep my eyes open for something cheaper. Whatever you want, all top-notch and in full working order. What do you say?"

This wasn't part of the operational plan and I wondered how much I could put on my expenses form before the Centre started getting shirty with me.

Detlef mistook my hesitation for miserliness and started listing prices. "Get you a mono-radio and cassette-player for a hundred. Or a transistor radio for fifty?"

"West?" I asked him.

Detlef didn't think that was worth an answer, of course he meant Deutsche Marks—not a lot he could do with our money back home in West Berlin.

We agreed he'd bring a second-hand sound system for me to look at and, with a clap on my shoulder, Detlef went back to his lorry.

The negotiations with Detlef had broken the ice with my colleagues and when I joined them again at the brazier, the old man to my left offered me a cigarette.

"What's wrong with getting a wireless from RFT? That's what I want to know," he griped.

"You ever seen anything like this in the shops?" Erich held up his new possession. "If it were up to Bert here, we'd still be winding our gramophones by hand. But you can trust Detlef. He can get other good stuff, too, not just music systems." He gave me a wink.

"Somebody oughta tell the authorities," Bert mumbled into his moustache.

The way he said it told me he didn't think it his job to do so.

7
GALLUN

That evening, I wrote up my report by hand. I included the details of persons I'd had contact with and suggested codenames for them.

When I'd finished, I read through what I'd written, double checking for any slips that might land me in trouble, then folded the thin paper twice lengthwise and rolled it up tight. I pushed it into an empty film canister and hid it behind a wooden plank in the wainscoting.

I pushed the board back and screwed the dado rail into place, smearing a little dirt from the flower pots into the head of the screw to mask any scratches from the screwdriver.

Satisfied with the hiding place, and desperate for another beer, I got my MZ motorcycle out of the shed.

The marketplace in Zossen was practically empty and I parked the bike outside a bar that was still open, even though it was nearly midnight.

It was the usual kind of place: stagnant cigarette smoke hanging over brightly lit chipboard bar and tables. The kind of place that sucked any lust for life from you. The only high spirits here were those distilled and bottled in Nordhausen.

I sat at the bar and ordered a beer, checking out the customers in the mirror behind the bottles of schnapps and brandy. The usual clientele: the dipsos out back, and at the front, the married couple frowning at the stained surface of their table.

I shifted my attention to the beer in front of me, trying to drink myself into a good mood. I was doing grunt work at the tip and doing grunt work in the evening when I wrote up my reports. There was nothing here for me to find out—a bit of smuggling, so what? It was all about as interesting as a guess-the-pumpkin's-weight contest at the allotment colony. That was bad news for me if I wanted to find something with which I could impress Captain Funke enough to make him transfer me out of here.

After a couple of beers, I decided I'd had enough. This place had less atmosphere than a Mitropa station buffet after the last train had left. I paid off the barkeeper and returned to my bike.

It was still raining.

8
ZOSSEN

A Soviet armoured car sputtered along in front of me.

I throttled back. Those things travelled in convoy and I had no chance of overtaking them on a country road like this. But as the BRDM-2 edged around a bend, I could see the road ahead of it was clear.

I slowed further, allowing some distance to develop. A Soviet armoured vehicle out by itself was unusual and that was enough to make me curious. Bearing in mind the medicinal effect curiosity had on the cat's health, I doused my headlights and held back.

We rattled over the cobbles of the village of Schöneiche and where the road forked, the light tank took the lane to the left, around the back of the landfill site.

I matched my speed to the Russians', then closed the throttle even further as they took us down the marshy lane. After a kilometre, we were at the edge of the waste tip. The fence was to my left and ahead of me the lights of the armoured car glimmered through the trees.

I braked gently as I splashed through a deep puddle, then, feeling the back wheel twist underneath me, I eased off the brake lever and steered into the skid, eyes fixed on the lane ahead. The back wheel bucked as it went over a pothole, the tires gripped again and the bike righted itself.

A few seconds, that was as long as it took to get the bike back under control, but by the time I could look up, the Russians had gone. I opened the throttle and leant into the next corner, underbranches from pines thrashing at my arms as my bike mounted the rise. I came to a stop at the top.

There were no vehicle lights in sight.

I switched off the engine and took my helmet off, turning my head this way and that, trying to hear above the whisper of the rain and the whistle of the wind in the pine trees.

There it was, off to my left, the heavy thud of a diesel engine, the sound coming from the landfill.

I wheeled the bike under the trees, left my helmet on the seat and layered branches over the top. Brushing pine needles over my tire tracks as I went, I headed back the way I'd come and went in search of the Russians.

I soon found where the armoured car had left the lane. The double fence at the edge of the dump had been mown down on some previous occasion, bushes and saplings were uprooted and flattened.

Navigating by the light of the moon, I climbed through the broken fence and up the mound of rubbish. My feet sank into the debris, broken glass glimmered like fake diamonds in the dull moonlight.

Walking in the compacted tyre tracks was a bit easier—obvious once I'd worked it out—and I made good progress up the slope, soon spotting the BRDM a hundred metres from the crest of the ridge.

Headlights glared over the wasteland, the damp piles of waste paper cast long shadows. The commander stood next to one of the hatches, watching as his three men, dressed in service uniforms, sifted through the old newspapers and magazines. I fumbled the field glasses from my pack and focussed on the searchers. One of the men was stumbling at the double towards the armoured car, his chest heaving out puffs of condensed breath. He saluted and handed his commander a magazine.

I couldn't make out the title, but the large area of flesh colour told me all I needed to know.

The soldier ran back to his comrades and the NCO used his sleeve to wipe some mud from the cover before leafing through the dirty mag. Meanwhile, I carefully made my way along the ridge, further away from the Russians and their exit path.

I watched as three more magazines were added to the pile next to the hatch. A search for skin mags seemed to be the extent of their mission, and reluctant to be caught peeping, I decided on tactical withdrawal.

I'd taken cover by a broken pram, but as I moved out from behind it, my foot slipped as the rubbish beneath my feet shifted. Trying not to slide down into the gunk, I stood up, arms outstretched for balance. I didn't make any noise, but the sliding detritus did. My heel knocked a can, the dull strike clanging clear above the rain.

I held my breath and watched the Russians who, blinded by their vehicle's headlamps, couldn't see me in the darkness beyond.

The commander scrambled up the turret and leaned through the hatch. He had the searchlight pointed in my direction before I could drop to the ground.

With the searchlight pinning a target on my back, I stepped out over the slope above the lane. My boots scudded through trash, I leant forward, allowing gravity to do its work, pulling me down the embankment.

Orders were shouted, I heard the heavy diesel engine coughing as they tried to get it to start, then the headlights strobed the terrain as the armoured car manoeuvred around. I didn't look back, but the clattering of boots told me the Russian soldiers were right behind me.

I was already halfway down the slope, skipping and slipping down the unstable layers of newspapers, packaging and abandoned household goods. I could already see the outline of the ripped fence in the moonlight, beyond that a stand of pines, then the lane.

Behind me, the Russians had stopped shouting, but I could hear their jagged breathing and the clanking and squelching of their boots sinking into the slop. Further back was the sawing pitch of the engine as the BRDM manoeuvred its way over the top of the slope.

The moonlight that had been so bright outside hardly seemed to penetrate the rubbish tip and when a hollow seemed to open up just a metre in front of me I had no choice but to attempt to jump over it. Slamming my foot down on a sheet of metal at the edge of the crater, I had to trust it wouldn't slip away from me.

It held.

I pushed off, launching myself over the shallow depression.

I cleared the gap and landed on my other foot.

I staggered, pitching forward, trying to regain my balance— one foot on firm ground, the other still poised in mid-air— when whatever I had landed on crumpled. I came down hard, feeling the skin of my knee part.

I looked over my shoulder, one of the soldiers was just a few metres behind me.

9
SCHÖNEICHE

I was back on my feet again, sprinting down the last of the slope and through the fence, into the shadows under the trees. I spared another glance over my shoulder, one of the soldiers was bent over, arm reaching downwards, the second Soviet wasn't to be seen. As the armoured car crested the ridge above, the headlamps punctured the darkness around me.

I crossed the lane and slowed down, easing into the trees and sidling through the narrow shadows. Another glance behind me as the engine pitch changed, the two soldiers were climbing aboard, they held fast as the armoured car continued to lurch down the slope.

I paced a few more metres into the shelter of the woods before moving sideways. Squint over my shoulder: the Russians were through the fence and slewing onto the lane. The turret mounted searchlight was pivoting around, lighting up the woods around me. I shrugged my pack off to reduce my silhouette and stood sideways behind a pine, offering as narrow a target as I could.

As the Russians came alongside, not twenty metres away, the light flickered in my direction. Wet trunks behind me glistened brightly, the shadows of the trees in front of me stroked the landscape as I held my breath, face turned away from the lamp.

The armoured car had stopped, the light swept through the trees again, shadows crossed in front of the lamp.

As the beam swept past, I peered around the side of the

trunk, one of the soldiers was heading back down the lane, rifle held at the ready. Another paced in front of the vehicle, kicking the sparse bushes to either side.

The shadows cast by the searchlight stretched and swung past me. I peered around the trunk, the BDRM was twenty metres ahead of me now. As I watched, I became aware of laboured breathing. I turned to see the dark grey of a figure, ten or so metres from me, rifle held loosely.

Without haste, I stretched my arms out to either side, showing my hands were empty. The soldier came closer, rifle still held low, but ready. We were close enough to see each other more clearly now, darker shadows for eyes and mouth. He looked young. Perhaps a ghost, their name for young lads in the first year of conscription.

We stood like that for seconds that ticked by like hours, each watching the other, each as frightened as the other. My eyes focussed on his left hand, it was lifting the rifle into position, his right elbow shifting to accommodate the movement. We were no more than three metres apart, could I reach him, knock aside the barrel of his rifle before he shot me?

The soldier's left hand released its grip on the Kalashnikov and with a flick of the wrist he shouldered the rifle.

Without a word, he turned away and disappeared into the darkness.

I waited until I could no longer hear the thumping of their engine and, finally, when the only sounds that reached me where the sighing of the trees and the sputtering of the rain, I returned to the motorbike.

I stood for a long time, listening for their engine, but it had long since faded into the night

10
SCHÖNEICHE

The gaffer was over the moon when I limped into work the next day.

"You're telling me you're pulling a sickie? Three days you've been here and you're ready for a holiday?" He watched me critically, hands on hips. "Pull up your trouser leg, I need to see this."

I pulled at the blue material, easing it over the swelling knee.

"How'd you do that, then?"

"Slipped yesterday, cut myself."

"So it's infected, big surprise. You put anything on it? Antiseptic's in the first-aid box at the gatehouse. In fact, stay there today. Harry will show you what to do."

Harry was from works security and like works security all over the Republic, he wore a standard police uniform with a patch reading *Betriebsschutz* on the arm.

He welcomed me in and fetched the bandage box from under his desk.

"Your jabs up to date?" he asked as he handed over the Sepso-tincture.

A lorry drove in and Harry checked the paperwork as I dribbled antiseptic on my knee. A jagged gash showed where I'd fallen last night and despite the inflammation, it didn't look too bad. Plus, it got me an easy day in the gatehouse—the best place to observe movements in and out of the site.

I laid a gauze dressing over the wound and bandaged it in place then joined Harry at the slidey window.

"Right, here's how it works. I check the driver's paperwork. If it's all in order I pass it on to you. Depending on what it is they're carrying you direct them to the right place." He handed me a rough sketch of the site, different zones marked for household refuse, liquid waste, construction waste, excavation material. "These forms here are for the weights—registration number, driver's name, waste type and weight."

The next lorry arrived and we all had a chance to check I was up to the job.

When it drove off, Harry slid the window shut on the fumes and the dust. "Coffee?"

I nodded and watched him put a heating coil into a jug of water then plug it in. He spooned out ground coffee into two mugs then sat back to wait for the water.

Before the coffee was ready, another truck had pulled up. Harry had the window open even before the hydraulics had gasped.

The driver got out of his cab and stood outside the gatehouse as Harry checked the documents. He handed me the lading bill and I copied the details into my forms then checked the reading from the weighbridge.

While I was doing that I kept the truck driver on the edge of my vision. He was gesticulating at Harry, his head bobbing in my direction. I turned slightly, ostensibly to enter the weight on the forms, but really so I could catch my colleague's reaction.

Harry was shaking his head.

I directed the driver where to dump and Harry and I went back to watching the water boil.

Detlef turned up while Harry had his snout in his coffee cup and I was dividing up a slice of cake my landlady had given me. Turns out she's not as bad as I thought.

I put the cake down and limped after Harry who was already pulling the window open.

"Got your feet under the table already?" Detlef shouted over his engine. "I'll have the radio for you on Monday. You can take a look, if you like what you see then we'll talk dough."

It was my turn to shake my head and look meaningfully at my colleague, pretending to be unsure about Harry's reliability.

Detlef laughed, took his papers back and drove off towards the part of the site I'd directed him to.

When Harry slid the window shut again there was silence. I could feel his eyes on me as I hobbled back to my cake and his scrutiny didn't stop once he'd sat down next to me. He slurped his coffee, looking at me over the rim of his cup. I pretended not to notice.

After a minute or two of this, he put his mug down. "What's Detlef bringing you?"

"Detlef?"

"Fine. That's how you want to play it." Harry stood up and took his seat by the window. He stared down the lane, counting orange lorries.

After finishing my coffee and cake, I joined my colleague at the window. I pretended to examine the sketch of the landfill site, looking out the window and comparing what I could see to the markings on the paper.

"It's OK, you know," Harry tried again. "We all do it."

"Do what?"

"You know. They bring us the odd thing. The parties."

"Parties?" If I sounded surprised it was because I was. But I was pleased, Harry was trying to reassure me that it was safe to talk—made a change from the usual trick of me persuading my informants to talk.

"Yeah, the lads from West Berlin bring a few crates of beer, we have a bit of a knees up."

"Regular, like?" I pasted shock on my face. Had to get it just right, overdo it and Harry would clam up.

"Whenever the mood takes them." Harry looked wistful. He was a bit older than me, too old to look wistful about parties with the class enemy.

"He's bringing me a radio," I told him.

"Like the one he got for Erich? I saw that. Nice bit of kit."

"Not as expensive as Erich's. Just a mono-cassette-radio."

"Don't let him rip you off, that's all I can say." Harry tried out a wise expression, but it just made him look like he'd had a stroke.

"Haven't got much choice, have I?"

"You met Richard yet? He'll sort you out, too."

The conversation was interrupted as a few lorries queued to leave the site. Harry checked the paperwork without enthusiasm and I watched as Detlef pulled away from the gatehouse and parked next to the Intershop a few metres away. He got out of his cab and went inside.

"Are we allowed in there?" I asked Harry, nodding at the duty-free shop.

"Put it this way," Harry sucked his moustache. "Nobody's ever told me not to, but I've never been in."

One of those unwritten rules, he meant. There was no need for a sign, we could be expected to know where we belonged.

"Tell me about Richard," I asked as Harry shut the window against the breeze that was wafting landfill smells into the gatehouse.

"One of them what comes over from West Germany. Drives a white truck, not like the orange ones from West Berlin. Hang around long enough and he'll introduce himself."

I thought of my first lorry driver yesterday. It was a white tipper, from West Germany, but the driver hadn't even bothered to say hello.

"Mainly deals with the Russians, does Richard."

"What do they buy?" I asked.

"Best not ask. That's my motto, 'specially when it comes to the Friends."

Harry didn't have much to say after that. It was as if he'd talked himself out. For the rest of the evening, all I heard from him were greetings to familiar lorry drivers.

That's not to say the day was wasted. When Harry went for a piss-break I had a look at his paperwork. The same drivers cropped up again and again, two, sometimes three times a day. Early shift then late shift. Pretty regular. But there were one or two West Berlin drivers that had only turned up once or twice this month.

Before I could check further back, Harry had returned. I shuffled my own papers around a bit, making sure to look bored, but Harry wasn't bothered. He plugged in his heating coil and hung it over the edge of the jug.

"Coffee," he said.

It was a statement, not a question.

11
BERLIN TREPTOW

Captain Funke sat behind his desk, fingering my report.

"Still nothing about the Intershop?" he asked, straightening the papers.

"Nothing to report as yet, Comrade Captain."

It was Sunday morning and I'd made the journey into Berlin for this meeting. Funke had kept me waiting in the corridor for an hour and now I was standing to attention in his office, trying to keep my weight off the bad leg.

"I sent you there to find out what was happening at the Intershop," Funke's steel-blue eyes threw a few icicles at me, then he carried on reading. "A radio?" he asked when he got to that bit. "A Western radio?"

"A price has been agreed with the criminal smuggler Spindler Detlef. The purchase of illegally imported goods is necessary for purposes of conspiration and to allow contact with persons of operational interest."

Funke wasn't enthusiastic, but he signed a chit and slid it over the desk towards me. I stepped forward and picked it up. A requisition order for two hundred Westmarks.

"And what do you expect us to do with these samples?" Funke used his silver fountain pen to tap one of the jars of waste I'd scooped from the West Berlin lorries' deliveries. That was as close as he wanted to get to the contents.

"Thank you, Comrade Second Lieutenant," he said when he realised I didn't have any suggestions. "Concentrate your efforts on the political-operational penetration of the

Intershop." It sounded like a dismissal.

I raised an eyebrow at Funke, who nodded. He was now using a long ruler to poke the sample jars on his desk.

I saluted and about-turned.

I was back in my office, fishing a glass from the bottom drawer when the door began to open.

No knock. That meant brass. I was already on my feet by the time the office door had fully opened.

"At ease, Comrade Second Lieutenant."

A major stepped inside. He sat himself in my visitor's chair and made an impatient gesture with a hand: sit down.

"Your report on the drivers," he said. "Those who don't come every day. Don't mention them again."

"Yes, Comrade Major," I snapped out, wondering how this unknown officer knew about the contents of my report.

"And the Russians. I want no more about what our Soviet brothers might be up to—understand?"

"Yes, Comrade Major," I repeated.

"Good. Otherwise, continue as you were. Scare Funke with more toxic samples, by all means. Tell him about leachate in the groundwater, tell him the locals have the plague—you can even give him some intelligence on that awful woman who manages the Intershop. But don't bother him with any more details about any irregular drivers or the Russians." The major was leaning back in his chair, feeling comfortable.

I was on the other side of the desk, feeling uncomfortable. I had questions but I knew I shouldn't expect any answers. "Comrade Major, permission to speak?"

"You have a question, ask it. No need to stand to attention."

"Comrade Major, the operational plan-"

"Stick to the bloody operational plan. Uncover enough unsavoury goings-on to satisfy your superior, but I require separate reports. I'm interested in those drivers and the Russians. I want to know what contact they have with each other. I want the when and how and why—that information is for me and only me."

Now that we'd broken the ice, the major let me have a few more details. I was to call him Major Blecher and he was from Main Department VIII, which didn't tell me much: HA VIII is responsible for searches, both for people and of premises. If you're looking for someone or something, if you want somebody tailed and evidence found or planted, you ask VIII to do it for you.

The major told me a few other things, but nothing particularly useful—I got as much background as a Thälmann Pioneer would get before a school trip to the zoo. He told me this was a strictly no-contact reconnaissance and otherwise confined himself to arranging contact points, dead drops and the usual mildewed pep-talk.

At the end of it all, I just had those two cornerstones—the irregular bin-lorry drivers and Soviet soldiers.

"Do this well, Reim and we'll see what we can do to tidy up your mess." The major was generous, not least with what he didn't say. I didn't need a translator to understand the veiled threats so typical of the Firm: do this badly and I'd end up back in Hohenschönhausen slammer.

"If I'm to watch Soviet troops, well, what about liaison with the KGB?" I enquired, feeling like I didn't have anything to lose by asking.

"No liaison."

"They don't know about this operation?"

"If the Russians catch you, you're on your own."

"Yes, Comrade Major." I stood up as he left my office, then sank back into my chair.

As my hand took itself off to the bottom drawer in search of glass and bottle, my mind jangled. Another operation off the books, I was thinking. Look where the last one got me.

Other people talk about being bothered by deja vu, I was being deafened by the civil-defence sirens in my head.

12
SCHÖNEICHE

The next week I was on early shift, starting at 0600 hours.

The gaffer took one look at me on Monday morning and sent me to the gatehouse. "You're no good to us with an injury —you need to take more care," he mumbled as I hinked past him.

Harry was there already, reading his newspaper. "Make yourself comfortable, lad," he told me. "The deliveries won't be here for another half hour."

"Been thinking about what you said about Richard," I began.

"Oh, aye?" Harry put the newspaper down and plugged his water heater into the socket. I noticed he had two mugs at the ready.

"I might have a chat with him, see what he can bring me."

Traffic was heavier than on Saturday and I spent the whole shift by the window.

From there I had a good view of the Intershop entrance. About a third of the lorries stopped, drivers coming back out with a few bottles of beer, a pack or two of cigarettes. Only once did I see a driver emerge with a box of spirits. He crawled underneath his trailer and when he reappeared the cardboard box was empty. He hurried into the shop again and five minutes later he crawled underneath with the same box.

From the way he was handling it, it looked much lighter this time.

"Cigarettes," said Harry over my shoulder. "Every so often you hear about customs in West Berlin doing a proper search when they cross the border. Driver gets off with a fine. Most of the time nobody cares what they take home. Our lot are happy about it, brings them the valuta." He rubbed thumb and forefinger together.

"What else do they sell in there?" I asked, still watching the entrance to the Intershop.

"Alcohol, cigarettes, coffee." He counted them off on his fingers. "Perfume. Anything the self-respecting trucker might need."

Anything with a high tax-rate that a trucker could take home, he meant. Buy it duty-free, sell it down the local in West Berlin.

Everyone wins, except the West German tax office. And who cares about them?

The truck driver emerged from under his trailer, chucked the empty box into the corner by the shop door and drove off. I looked at the forms in front of Harry and memorised the driver's name and licence plate.

We were busy for the next twenty minutes or so, a queue of lorries appeared on the lane, waiting to be processed. By the time we'd cleared them, Harry was no longer in a talkative mood.

That was fine by me, I was watching another lorry come in. This was different from the others, plain blue curtain sides and its destination wasn't the tip, but the Intershop.

I told Harry I needed a cigarette and ignoring his reassurances that it was OK to smoke inside, I left the gatehouse and headed for the back of the Intershop.

A fork-lift had appeared and was waiting while the driver pulled back the sides of the trailer. A woman stood by the back door. Mid-thirties, dyed blonde hair cut and permed into a mullet, wearing a white shop-apron. She'd had the same idea as me and was smoking a cigarette.

I wandered over and asked for a light. She gave me a box of matches without taking her eyes off the truck.

"I've just started here," I said.

"I can tell, the dirt looks like it'll still wash off," replied the manager of the Intershop.

Heidrun Bahrmann was her name, I knew because I'd seen her file.

I chuckled appreciatively, but her attention was still on the delivery. The fork-lift was pulling out a pallet of stretch-wrapped boxes.

"Make sure your eyes don't get bigger than your wallet, young man," the woman advised me.

"You the boss here?"

"What's it to you?"

"Nothing, just finding my feet. Getting to know the colleagues."

"Listen, *colleague*. You work over there, I work over here. Different places. Right, cigarette break over." She followed the fork-lift into the back of her shop.

As I walked back to the gatehouse, Detlef overtook me in his lorry. I joined him at the window to the gatehouse and watched as Harry completed the formalities, including filling in my form for me.

"Fifteen minutes. At the plant shed," the driver told me as he swung back up into his cab.

"Go on then, it'll take you that long to limp that far," Harry gave me a look I couldn't work out.

The gaffer was in the garage, in his reclaimed armchair, reading the *Bild*. He looked up from his Western newspaper and decided to ignore me as I hung around in the entrance.

Detlef didn't need long to dump his load and come back down the rubble track. His truck hissed to a halt in front of me and Detlef jumped down. He reached back into the cab and pulled out a plain cardboard box. I unpacked the radio and held it up in front of me, doing my best to look impressed. There were a couple of scratches on the bottom and the screw that held the aerial needed tightening.

"Nice one," I told Detlef as I handed the money over.

"Pleasure doing business," he replied. "Anything else you need, just let me know."

"What else can you get hold of?"

"All sorts. If you can name it, there's a good chance I can get hold of it."

I picked the radio up again and examined it. "Well, what else do people want?"

Detlef was looking at the Brigade Leader now, who was lost in his newspaper. "If there are any particular magazines you want," he said with a wink.

He was already turning away, I had time for just one last question: "Special mags? The kind the Russians like?" Detlef didn't reply. He gave me a nod from up in the cab and put the lorry into gear.

"Shouldn't ask too many questions," said the gaffer, still hiding behind his newspaper. "Tends to make folks nervous."

13
SCHÖNEICHE

Richard turned up just before shift end.

"Lucky we're still letting you in," Harry joked. "Another ten minutes and you'd have to stand around while we handed over to the late shift."

I directed the West German where to dump and just as he was about to climb into his cab I asked him a question: "I've heard say, you can help out. You know, with stuff?"

Richard hesitated, one foot on a step, hand reaching up to grab the rail next to his cab door. His eyes flicked towards Harry. Harry looked at me, then gave Richard a slow nod.

"Another time," the driver said, getting into his cab and shutting his door.

"I thought you'd just got your radio from Detlef?" asked Harry as he slid the window shut.

"We've all got friends, haven't we? Could be they might be interested in a sound system."

"You don't hang around, do you?" Harry said as he busied himself with his paperwork.

Another late delivery arrived and Harry muttered something about making them wait for the next shift to start, but really we had no choice but to process them.

A tall man, average build, a bit young for his tight, curly hair to be so grey. He wore blue overalls rather than the orange ones all the other West Berlin drivers had.

Standing outside the window, he shoved his papers through

the gap and lit a cigarette. Lucky Strike, same as the driver on the first day.

When he opened his mouth to feed the stick in, his lips had trouble stretching over grey teeth. It was like he'd been allocated too many of them.

He sucked on the cigarette, paying more attention to the scenery than to either of us.

After we'd finished copying the details out and weighing his load, Harry gave him his papers back. Normally at this point there's a thank you, at least a grunt but this driver just took the paperwork and climbed back into his truck. I looked at the registration number on my forms. It was one of the irregular drivers.

"Friendly fellow—don't think I've seen him before," I fished.

"That's Olli Schraber. He's a relief driver. Comes by once or twice a month." Harry wasn't particularly interested.

The safe was open and I was about to put my paperwork in, but after checking Harry was still at the window, I leafed through the forms he had already filed. Didn't see anything worth mentioning in a report.

"Listen, Harry, do you mind if I get off on time? I want to get to the *Poliklinik* in Mittenwalde. I should let a doctor take a look at this leg." I pointed at my knee. It was healing nicely, but nobody had asked to see it today, so they weren't to know. "Can I leave you to do the handover to the next shift?"

Harry grunted good-naturedly and I left the gatehouse.

I sat astride my MZ, waiting opposite the Intershop. When Olli Schraber came through the gates of the landfill and turned down the lane, I turned the key and gunned the engine.

The truck headed north, towards Mittenwalde. Suited my cover story just fine.

I set off, slowly, leaving a fair bit of distance between us as Schraber headed around the Mittenwalde bypass and onto a smaller road. So far, so normal. He was taking one of the approved routes back to Berlin.

Strange thing was, he was travelling even more slowly now, just over thirty kilometres an hour. Didn't he want to get home? We passed a few outlying houses and a couple of collective farms, Schraber maintaining his low speed while I maintained a decent distance—it's hard to lose a bright orange twenty-tonne truck on a country road.

A woodland was coming up, the road curving around as it dived through the middle. As the truck disappeared behind the trees, I opened the throttle, not wanting to let the lorry out of sight for too long.

As I came out of the curve, I had to lean straight back out again, Schraber's lorry was parked by the side of the road. No choice but to overtake.

As I finished the manoeuvre, I checked my mirror, saw Schraber crossing to the other side of the road. A hundred metres further, I took another look: he was standing by a tree, looking like an old man having trouble pissing.

Pulling in at the next collective farm, I turned the bike around and stayed out of sight behind a shed, engine running. It was ten minutes before I heard the lorry's engine dopplering towards me. It rumbled past and after giving it a head start, I eased out of the farmyard and followed Schraber.

We were soon on the F96, the trunk road that leads straight to the border checkpoint set up for rubbish lorries crossing back into West Berlin. I edged closer to the truck when we neared the junction with the Berliner Ring motorway and again as we passed through Mahlow, fearful of losing him.

But the town limits of Mahlow was where I had to let him go. The final few hundred metres before the border were closed to citizens of the Republic, but that was all fine: from this point onwards the truck would be under constant observation by the Border Troops and the checkpoint control staff. I checked my watch: 1442. It had taken Schraber over forty minutes to make a journey that I guessed would normally take half that time.

14
GALLUN

On Tuesday morning I went for a walk before my shift started. It was still dark, but the mist shimmered above the fields like dead souls. Perfect weather.

At the edge of the village, on the road to Motzen, I stepped onto the verge and played the role of man urinating against tree. I had a look around, nobody out and about this grey morning. Under cover of pretending to do up my flies, I dropped a broken plastic pen on the ground and nudged it into a deep fork of the roots with my foot.

A hundred metres further on, I took another cautious look around. Still no-one in sight. Satisfied, I pulled a thin polythene bag out of my pocket, no different from the hundreds that blow out of the landfill and litter the landscape. I wound it around a low branch of a bush, easily seen by anyone driving along the road.

Satisfied with the constitutional effects of my stroll, I decided to continue with the exercise and walked all the way to work.

"How's your leg today," the Brigade Leader was waiting for me by the gate.

"Healing nicely, thanks." I'd enjoyed hanging out with Harry in the warmth, but political-operational penetration couldn't be done from the gatehouse.

"Ever driven one of them?" The gaffer pointed to a tracked bulldozer.

"Basic military service as a tank commander."

"You know how it works, then. Two levers: starting position, one and two. Another lever for the blade. Reckon you can manage that? Right, go to the special waste sector. Bert will show you what to do."

I spent the shift shovelling household waste over asbestos cement sheets. The orange lorries from West Berlin turned up, emptied the asbestos into pits and I'd push dirt and rubbish over the top.

Out of sight, out of mind.

After shift end, I rolled my motorbike out of the widow's driveway and went for a spin. I took the road to Mittenwalde and turned off towards Zossen, parking up in the marketplace and entering the same bar I'd visited last week.

The place was just as dead as last time, everyone in their place, the drunks were still quietly getting pissed, the married couple still weren't talking to each other and the bartender still wasn't pleased to see me.

I took my time, sipping an acid beer as slowly as I could and watched the clock. When the little hand got to ten, I slid off my stool and went out the door marked by an arrow and a sign reading *Abort*. The corridor beyond led to the backyard.

Wooden crates of bottles and empty barrels stood around in the shadows, but nothing was moving, no shadows were breathing.

A gate took up most of the wall at the end of the yard and I went to check that first. It was bolted from the inside. Reassured, I entered the toilets. They were in an outhouse opposite the gate—I could tell I was in the right place because they stank of stale piss and fresh *Wofasept* disinfectant.

The sound of the door opening was masked by the splashing of condensation dripping off pipes, but I was waiting, and saw one of the alcoholics as he staggered in. His small eyes, set well back below a fringe of greasy hair, flicked around. Once he was sure we were alone, he stood up straight and extended his right hand. Not for a shake, but to receive the package of reports I had for him.

I left him in the toilets and went through the bar on my way back to my bike.

The next morning I visited my tree again. The broken pen was lying between the roots, just as I'd left it. Bending down to tie my shoelace, I scooped it into the palm of my hand, depositing it in my pocket as I stood up.

Back home, I fetched a pair of fine tweezers from my wash bag and pulled a roll of paper from the inside of the pen. I eased the paper flat so I could read the message.

1530h, Pablo-Neruda-Str. 57

An address in the Allende Quarter, down in Köpenick. Presumably a safe house, because it wasn't one of the Ministry's many office complexes.

The appointment was timed so that I could finish my shift and get to Berlin easily. Somebody was keeping tabs on my working hours.

I made good time on the Dresden-Berlin autobahn but got snarled up by the river in Köpenick. Even on a motorbike, it was hard to find a way through the dense traffic on the bridge over the River Dahme and through the *Altstadt.*

Parking my bike on Pablo-Neruda-Strasse, I threaded my way through the maze of concrete flats that was the first phase of the Allende Quarter. I found my entrance and, ignoring the lift, took the stairs up to the seventh floor where I knocked on the second door from the left.

Major Blecher himself let me in. Off to one side of the vestibule, a young man with short back and sides—NCO material if I knew anything about anything—was busy with a coffee machine in the kitchen. Coats hung on hooks in the hall, below them shoes and winter boots stood to attention.

The major beckoned me into the living room and I closed

the door. Blecher remained standing, which meant I couldn't take a seat myself. Several folders were stacked on the coffee table. A plant pot had been pushed to one side, as had the knick-knacks of everyday life: an ashtray, magazines, a box of matches. This flat had been borrowed, the tenants sent out to spend a few hours away from home while the Firm helped themselves to their living space.

"Good work," Major Blecher told me. "You've been there less than a week and you're already making progress."

I didn't contradict him, but that didn't mean I was enthusiastic about my progress. Russians looking for porn mags in the night, some petty smuggling and a lorry driver that stopped for a piss on the way home. Not much to show for my work and certainly not enough to facilitate my return to civilisation.

"We've decided to call your driver Oskar. From now on, the driver Schraber will be referred to as codename Oskar," the Major was still being excitable, but I had no objections, the major could call the lorry driver whatever he wanted.

"I want you to look at these," Blecher pointed at the folders on the table. "Tell me what you think."

I got to work on the files.

I ignored the NCO who brought us coffee and I ignored Blecher, who was pacing around in front of the window. His restlessness made me nervous but it wasn't my place to tell him. Instead, I tried all the harder to concentrate on the paperwork in front of me.

"Well?" the major asked when I closed the last file.

"There's a pattern," I told him. I turned my notes around so he could see the dates and times I'd written down. "The driver Schraber Olli always turns up around 1400 hours."

"Codename Oskar," the major corrected me. "What's your point?"

"Oskar, like all the other West Berlin waste truck drivers, uses the border crossing point on the old F96 at Mahlow-"

"What of it? That's the only border crossing they can use."
The major was impatient, but I was used to dealing with brass.
Maybe they'd known everything at one time, but in my
experience you have to spell things out to them because
they're easily confused.

"The border crossing is open between 0600 and 2300, so the
Pass and Control Unit works two shifts-"

"And shift change is at 1400," said the major, finally
catching up.

"When Oskar leaves the territory of the GDR, his
paperwork is controlled by a different shift than when he
enters." Blecher studied the dates and times I'd written down,
nodding sagely. But he didn't notice the other pattern that I'd
uncovered.

"Schraber, or Oskar, does the delivery and returns a few
days later. Then we don't see him again for a while." I ringed
the different periods with my pen. "Delivery this day and one,
two or three days later there's another one. Absent two weeks
then twice in four days. Absent two months, two deliveries in
three days."

"Good work, Comrade *Unterleutnant* Reim. And what's the
significance of his movements?"

I had no idea.

15
GALLUN

I spent the evening at my dormer window. Bottle of beer in one hand, binoculars in the other, cigarette smoking itself in the ashtray.

This afternoon the major had focussed on Codename Oskar. I agreed we needed to take a closer look at the truck driver, but I didn't see the point of concentrating on him to the exclusion of all other activities. Why was Blecher so interested in Oskar? Had Blecher discovered this interest since he read my report on the driver's movements, or was my job to provide collateral for other reports on Oskar?

I remained by the window, watching the constant traffic. One truck every three minutes, thirteen hours a day, six days a week. But there was no point to what I was doing, I couldn't see the trucks' registration plates from this distance.

I was just killing time.

The next morning, instead of reporting for the early shift, I took the bike into Mittenwalde and showed my civilian identity card to the receptionist at the hospital.

She clocked the name and fetched an envelope from a drawer. The whole exchange took less than twenty seconds and happened without a word being spoken—that's the kind of official encounter I can live with.

Once outside, I opened the envelope and checked the green form inside. Sick note, courtesy of the major and valid for one week.

I dropped the note off at the landfill site on my way past. The gaffer wasn't pleased, but there it was, printed black on green: I needed to give my leg a rest.

The next village along the road is Kallinchen. In the summer, it's packed with tourists, enjoying a holiday on the banks of Lake Motzen, ignorant of the fact that toxic waste is being dumped just a few kilometres from where they like to go swimming.

At this time of year, you'll only find the locals in Kallinchen. And the Stasi. You won't actually get to see the lads from the Firm, but you'll hear them in the woods, gunning their engines around a race track and practising shooting from speeding vehicles.

Major Blecher must pull some weight, the way he'd organised a pass to the training ground. It's run by Main Department Personal Protection and they don't let just anyone into their little fiefdom in the forest.

I wasn't expecting them to roll out the red carpet and give me a private tour, but I was hoping for a quick shifty at the long wheel-base Volvos running in formation and doing co-ordinated hand-brake turns.

As it was, I didn't get much of a look around. I was fetched from the Control Post at the gate and taken to the vehicle park where I was entrusted with a Trabant.

I looked the car over, got in and fired up the engine. It was in good condition, caught first time and the engine settled down nicely without me having to put too much work into the choke.

Only problem was, the Trabi was so clean it shone like the buttons on an officer's dress uniform, but a quick spin through the woods and down some rutted lanes would take care of that.

★

There'd been some discussion about whether I could interview Control and Passport Unit personnel at the border crossing. In the end, Major Blecher decided against: I was undercover and being spotted anywhere near the border crossing would blow my cover if colleagues or West Berlin truckers should happen to recognise me.

Instead, the major promised I'd get a look at the interview protocols and would be informed immediately if anything came up that might be operationally relevant.

I stopped again in Mittenwalde, found a phone box and put a call through to Berlin. The news was that the truck driver Olli Schraber hadn't made the crossing yesterday or so far today. If he stuck to his usual pattern then we could probably expect him either this afternoon or tomorrow. Day after at the latest.

Which is why I spent the rest of the day parked outside one of the agricultural collective's milk farms.

I've had worse postings. This wasn't anything like lying in a waterlogged ditch for twelve hours straight or carrying out surveillance in a derelict factory in the middle of winter. Here I was, feet up in the farm office, staring out the window at the endless fields opposite. I could see the orange trucks go by, but there was no need for me to check registration numbers—I was sitting right beside a telephone and the moment Oskar crossed the border, that phone would ring.

16
MITTENWALDE

The call didn't come that day.

I went home at 2200 and returned the next morning at 0600, breakfast snap and thermos of coffee in my bag. I had to sit there for seven hours before the phone rang.

"Subject Oskar has arrived at the border crossing point," the Control and Passport commander told me. "Any instructions?"

"Allow him to pass normally."

I shrugged my coat on and went out to the Trabi. The pair of us went just a kilometre down the road, where I left the car by itself again, this time down a narrow lane behind some trees.

I jogged back to the road and found myself a dry ditch with plenty of undergrowth. I was within twenty metres of where Schraber had stopped the other day and you could say I had a hunch. Personally, I wouldn't go that far. I was here because I didn't know where else to begin the surveillance.

I trained my binoculars along the road, watching traffic come from the direction of the junction with the F96 main road.

There were a few cars, the odd East German truck, but the orange twenty-tonners from West Berlin were what I saw most of.

I checked my watch, Oskar wouldn't get here for at least another ten minutes, but that was fine. It gave me time to make myself comfortable. A truck passed, I'd made the plate while it was still more than three hundred metres away and was already waiting for the next one.

Another truck went by, then I got excited because I could see the plates of the one behind that: it was Oskar.

I lifted the binoculars to the windscreen, could just about make out the figure behind the wheel. I watched as he slowed down and pulled up, same place as last time.

He climbed out of his cab and crossed in front of his lorry, heading for the dense trees at the side. My binoculars swung around, I caught the back of his head. Grey curls peeked from below a cap. I tracked him into the thicket but then lost sight of him behind a stand of bushes.

I was stuck in my hide—he'd spot any attempt at following him. All I could do was stay here and practice being patient.

And there he was, not forty seconds later, coming back out of the trees.

I focussed the field glasses on his face, looking for any signs of nervousness, any clue of what he might have been doing in the woods. He'd taken his cap off and was picking his grey teeth with a fingernail as he went.

I watched him climb into the cab. There was something different about him, something physical. His gait was tighter than a minute or two ago. Perhaps his stride was shorter? Whatever he had been doing, it wasn't just having a piss in the woods—it had changed him. Stress can do that to you, you can keep your features as impassive as a portrait of the Comrade General Secretary, but your body will betray you.

Schraber drove off and I stayed in my ditch, scanning the woods on both sides of the road, watching for movement. Three trucks roared past, scattering sand and dust. A Trabant and a Wartburg ticked by. But from the woods, nothing.

I was in the middle of an age-old conundrum that spies all over the world face: Schraber had probably left a message or a package in the woods. Should I try to find it or wait around in the hope of identifying whoever might pop by to collect it?

Lying in the ditch, breathing in dust and fumes from the

traffic, I considered Schraber's activities. He always went to the landfill at this time of day. If this was a dead drop, the chances were it would be emptied soon since the delivery times were predictable. While I debated waiting for Schraber to return on his way back from Schöneiche, I heard a motorbike. It was the high pitch of a small, two-stroke engine, but that wasn't what caught my attention.

The whiny engine hadn't become gradually more insistent as it came up the road, like a mosquito circling in on you while you try to sleep. This engine had started up nearby.

The engine noise quickly grew in volume and I got a good view of it as it went past. A Simson S51, silver tank, newish model with the exhaust mounted higher than usual. I caught the registration—local plates.

The dead-drop had already been emptied.

There was a lull in the traffic and I took the opportunity to climb out of my ditch and walk along the road until I got to the point where Schraber had gone into the woods. The carpet of pine needles meant there were no clear imprints, but scuffed earth and broken twigs told the way.

About a hundred metres into the woods I found a pleasant place to sit and have a smoke. I could tell because of the butts spread out around the fallen tree.

There were two fresh ends and several more that were grey with damp. I took a series of photographs of the picnic spot, then examined the fresh cigarette ends more closely before bagging them up and stowing them in my rucksack. Lucky Strikes, an American brand popular in West Berlin. The same brand smoked by Oskar.

The whole set-up had me scratching my head. Schraber parks his truck at the side of the road and walks into the woods. Smokes three cigarettes and returns to the truck.

All in forty seconds.

I circuited the clearing again and now I had an idea of what to look for, it didn't take me long to find it: another track led away from the clearing. It followed an undulating course up the hill and in a dip I found a nice, clear boot print in the damp sand. I took several photos and stripped a few leaves from a struggling oak and hung them over a pine branch as a marker.

A couple of hundred metres further on, the track brought me back to the road, just around the curve from my temporary stake out. The earth and pine needles under the trees by the roadside had been kicked up by tyres. The same kind of tyres you find on a Simson S51.

Schraber hadn't serviced a dead drop—this was a person to person hand-over.

17
BERLIN KÖPENICK

The view from the borrowed flat was as boring as you'd expect.

Ten storeys of slab-build concrete flats across the courtyard and to either side. Kindergarten between the parked cars below. The place was deserted. There were no children playing outside, they'd all be marching and waving flags in the centre of Berlin.

I turned my attention back to the flat itself. The brown and white wallpaper that was threatening to give me a migraine. The brown and green carpet designed to induce nausea. I considered turning on the television in the corner but didn't want the major catching me with my feet up. Besides, the only thing on would be live footage from Karl-Marx-Allee and other parades around the country.

Day of the Republic, national holiday, and I was stuck in this stuffy flat. Still, it beat marching through Potsdam with my colleagues from the tip, waving wee flags and big banners at the District Party leadership.

So I was here, preparing myself for a conspirational meeting with Major Blecher. I mentally reviewed my operational requirements for the twentieth time: I wanted a mobile observation team stationed at the border crossing and I wanted to set up covert observation of the woods.

If I couldn't do that then the only other way of finding out what Oskar was up to was to go to West Berlin.

My file may have been marked *West Confirmed*, but being

in the Firm's bad books meant I had less chance of being allowed to travel to West Berlin than I had of finding a teetotal Soviet soldier.

The major walked into the living room—I hadn't heard the front door, but I managed to snap my back straight and salute before he had a chance to acknowledge my presence, so no harm done.

"As you were, Comrade Second Lieutenant," he murmured as he made himself comfortable on the couch. "Your report, please."

I filled him in on Oskar and his meeting with the person on the Simson and outlined my requests for operational forces for observation.

Blecher shook his head. Request dismissed.

There was a pause as he moved on the couch, as if he'd just discovered a spring poking through the ticking.

"Any idea who it was on the motorbike?" he asked once he'd got comfortable.

"I found several cigarette ends at the meet point, Lucky Strikes."

"American," the major said to himself. "Any other indications as to the identity of this person?"

"Only the registration number on the Simson S51. I haven't run a check on that yet."

Blecher raised a hand and the NCO that had been hovering in the background ever since I arrived moved into the limelight. I recited the registration number of the motorbike and the NCO made a note of it, clicked his heels, saluted and left the flat.

"We'll have that checked out. In the meantime, I've brought more reading material for you." The officer took several folders out of his briefcase, setting them on the coffee table in front of one of the chairs.

I sat myself down and opened the first file.

"Reports by an unofficial collaborator at the Schöneiche

landfill site?" I asked.

"Just because you're spending all your time keeping track of codename Oskar and his friends doesn't mean Captain Funke won't be expecting regular reports on activities at Schöneiche. Thought you might find something useful in there."

He was right. These files should hold enough intelligence for me to synthesise more information for reports to my superior. Rather than query the similarity to other reports, he'd be pleased that I was confirming earlier intelligence.

"Permission to take notes, Comrade Major?"

"Make them cryptic." Blecher pursed his lips.

I needed no more encouragement but got my notepad and pen out, jotting down names, relationships and events in an arcane code that I'd developed over the years.

My scribblings were interrupted by the return of the NCO. He did the whole saluting thing and handed the major a note.

Blecher read it, then folded the slip of paper and put it in his pocket.

"A local. No need for you to risk your cover on this, we'll follow it up and let you know if anything comes of it," said the major.

That had me scratching my head. Why couldn't he tell me who the registered keeper of the Simson was?

Having learned the hard way that it's rarely worth challenging a senior officer, I changed the subject. I could do a trace on the number plate myself later.

"Comrade Major, if we are restricted to mounting observations in areas away from the border crossing point, then the only way to continue this operation will be to initiate observation of Oskar in the operational area of West Berlin."

The major didn't stir. My remarks were nothing new to him, he'd already made his decision:

"If we have to send you to West Berlin to follow Oskar, then that is what we shall do."

18
BERLIN KÖPENICK

Now the major had made his decision, I was no longer sure I wanted to go to West Berlin.

When confronted with the choice of setting up a larger observation force here or sending me to the other side, he hadn't hesitated. That made me suspicious.

And why was the major so shy about revealing the owner of the motorbike? That was an angle I would have preferred to check out myself, and the first step would be to run the plates.

Except, now I thought about it, even checking the registration number might not be so straightforward. If I asked for the information from Berlin Centre, word could get back to Major Blecher.

I scratched my head a bit, then went in search of a phone box.

I held while my contact in the Potsdam police contacted central information on the other line.

Captain Lang was back with the answer within a minute.

"Simson S51, silver. Registered to Border Regiment 42," he said.

"Can you repeat that?"

Lang told me again but I'd heard him right the first time. GR42 was the regiment responsible for the sector of the border either side of the crossing point used by the waste trucks.

Now I understood Blecher's reluctance to tell me about the

owner of the bike—something like this needed to be reported to HA I, the department responsible for security within the armed forces. But if Blecher did that he would ignite a turf war between departments and there was no guarantee he would be able to keep hold of his case.

It also explained why Blecher would rather have me continue observation in West Berlin—Border Regiment 42 shares facilities with several other units in the National People's Army, with bases in several towns in the area. If the operation were to be expanded to include observation of border or army personnel then Main Department I would get wind of it. Once that happened there wouldn't just be a turf war at the Ministry, there'd be questions about why the major hadn't reported the situation.

The major had made clear his preference for an off-the-books operation in West Berlin with a single operative. I don't have to tell you that this isn't the way the Firm operates. And I don't have to tell you that after recent experiences I felt a little uneasy about getting involved in another unofficial op—being ordered to engage in under-the-radar activity was what had got me this plum job at a rubbish tip in the first place.

But this one had much more potential to be much worse, I told myself. I wasn't just tidying up after my Boss's affairs with unsuitable subjects, this time there were more players involved and once they all pitched in, they'd be shovelling their stakes onto the table, with my good self in the role of collateral.

19
SCHÖNEICHE

Schraber-alias-Oskar had made his second delivery and we had no way of knowing when his next run might be.

Once he crossed the border again, we could expect him a second time within a few days and that is when we could make our move.

Until then, and since my sick leave had already expired, I was back at the tip, sorting through the dregs of capitalism.

There was a shortage of operators for the tracked vehicles, so the Brigade Leader mostly had me on the bulldozer. Sitting in the cab kept me dry and out of the worst of the dust clouds. What's more, it meant I didn't have to physically handle any waste.

On the downside, I got to work with hazardous materials all day, every day.

At least Captain Funke was pleased with my reports. He enjoyed the fact that they mirrored so much of what he'd already read in the files. The additional information gained from observations of colleagues at the tip, not to mention their relationships outside of work, seemed to give my superior a false sense of progress.

For Funke, the highpoint was when I presented my report on one of the infamous 'parties' between tip workers and West Berlin lorry drivers. He had to sit down and light a cigarette on account of the excitement of it all.

The report had needed as much enhancing as a speech by

Yuri Andropov. The party at the tip had been about as lively as a Party conference, the only thing in its favour was it didn't last as long—the drivers had to be back in West Berlin and tucked up in bed before the border crossing closed for the night, and that's why the festivities started in the early afternoon.

I'd been on early shift but the gaffer asked me to put in a few hours overtime. The deliveries had bunched up in the first few hours of the late shift, rather than the usual steady spread through the afternoon and evening.

As soon as they'd got rid of their payload, the drivers headed over to the Intershop, returning with beer and spirits, plus chocolate, salted peanuts and other snacks.

We stood around the oil-drum brazier in the plant shed, drinking beer. Looking at the labels made me giddy—the brands were the same as those I drank at home: Schultheiss and Kindl, but this was beer brewed in the West by Western firms.

At least the schnapps didn't make me cross-eyed with confusion. Solid Western brands—Asbach Uralt, Mariacron, even some Bells and Grants Scotch were making the rounds.

You'll have guessed already that the fusel was the most exciting thing about the event. It was like a dance organised by the youth organisation. But instead of boys down one side of the hall and girls down the other, we had *Westler* sitting on one side of the brazier and us lot opposite.

The bottles made their way across the divide, promoting fraternal feelings between the political blocs. Heidrun, the Intershop manager, was enthusiastic about easing any remaining international tension. She was firmly ensconced on one of the driver's knees and had already accepted some perfume that she'd probably sold just an hour before.

Right now she was enjoying her role as party girl and was laying into a bottle of Malteser Aquavit. When it was time for the Westerners to head back to the border, the Intershop manager accompanied them as far as the gate.

I stood by the entrance to the garage smoking a Camel and watching Detlef take his gallant leave. Heidrun didn't use her handkerchief to wipe away her tears but I wouldn't have been surprised if she'd whipped it out to wave a tragic farewell to her West Berlin beau on his trusty orange steed.

After the truckers went, the beer soon dried up and the workers began to trickle homewards.

I didn't draw attention to myself by staying until the end, but from my bedroom window I could see the light in the garage burning until well after midnight. They must have hidden a bottle or two.

20
SCHÖNEICHE

Codename Oskar turned up again the week after the party. It was a Thursday afternoon when I found that out from Harry.

I'd made a point of buttering up the watchman, brought him a packet of coffee and visited him during my breaks. He probably thought I appreciated the oil heater he'd installed under his desk.

Conversation was sparse, Harry wasn't much of a talker and that suited me fine. One quiet afternoon, I amused myself by leafing through Harry's forms, commenting on the different loads.

And there was our Oskar: Olli Schraber, black on white in the book. He'd come in earlier that day and, true to form, he'd arrived just before 1400 hours and left just after. I checked my watch, another couple of hours until shift-end. After that, I'd get on the MZ, find a phone box and register Oskar's status, then go to the one or the other safe flat to wait for my handler.

I left work early, made the call from a phone box outside Schönefeld airport, then headed around the Berliner Ring autobahn.

It was longer that way round but I got to give the bike a bit of an airing. A final bit of freedom before I headed into the other half of the city.

The conspirational flat we were meeting at was in Pankow, not far from where the political brass used to have their digs on Majakowskiring. But this was a step down from what the bigwigs are used to: an old tenement block that had survived the war, just. And it hadn't seen much maintenance since.

I was holed up in a cold flat overlooking the backyard. Mounds of brown coal briquettes were scattered around under washing lines and I considered going down to fetch a bucketful. But I was keen to get started on the next stage of the operation and firing up the stove and making the flat cosy felt like a delay, even though I had to wait for whoever it was who would be handling me to turn up.

I checked my kit, there wasn't much of it: a suit and a couple of outfits of workman's clothes, a couple of watches, a pair of plain-lensed glasses, three different hats and three differently coloured jackets and coats.

I folded the clothes again and put them in a black Puma sports bag and put that in a green duffel sack. After all that activity I sat back and waited.

To while away the time, I tested myself on my legend: name, address, date of birth, religion, name of health insurers. Usual kind of thing.

It was the major himself who arrived half an hour later, dressed in civilian clothes. I did the whole stand-up-and-beg thing and he put me at ease. He had a map case with him and he opened it up to show me the route I'd take to get to the West.

"You'll be picked up by a Border Troops personnel carrier outside the swimming baths and be taken to the border near Wollankstrasse. From there you'll be shown the way by a Border Scout. The S-Bahn station itself is still on the territory of the capital of the GDR but access is only from West Berlin. While you remain at the station you're outside the jurisdiction of West Berlin police and counter-intelligence services."

I examined the map. As the major had said, the S-Bahn station was in a forward area, west of the Wall, but still within the political boundary of East Berlin: the actual border between East and West ran along the kerb of the street in front of the station.

"Return by the same route is possible every day after the last train. The station is staffed by Reichsbahn personnel based in the East. Make yourself known to them by 2105. Ask for the time of the next connection to the Botanical Gardens. You'll be told there's no S-Bahn service on that line. Then ask where you can catch the U-Bahn.

Your presence will be reported and you can return once the station personnel advises. In an emergency, return via Friedrichstrasse station at any time." He didn't have to say it but if I returned via Friedrichstrasse Station Border Crossing my arrival would be clocked by my own department and questions would be asked.

Best avoided.

The major shut the map case and pulled a slip of paper from his pocket, a West Berlin telephone number was written on it.

"Call this number when you're in the operational area. You'll be given further instructions. Contact in the same way once in every twenty-four hour period."

Blecher had a few more logistical details for me to get my head round but we had already agreed the overall operational plan when we last met in Köpenick. I was ready as I ever would be.

"Time for you go over the Wall." The major checked his watch. "Good luck."

21
BERLIN PANKOW

A military truck halted in front of Pankow Baths, the tailboard dropped and I climbed into the back, pulling the canvas cover down behind me as we set off. A tall border guard sergeant was waiting for me on the bench.

It wasn't yet six o'clock, but it was already dark and the sergeant was hard to make out in the back of the truck. He handed me a set of military fatigues—the usual dash-no-dash camouflage. I pulled them on and folded my dirty work clothes, packing them into my green duffel sack. By the time I was ready, the truck had stopped.

"We're about to enter the security strip. Entry is through a gate in the *Hinterland* wall. There are further gates in the signal fence and the border wall. I'll let you through these gates and leave you at the border wall where you'll change into Western clothing and leave the field uniform with me."

The sergeant's voice was toneless, his face expressionless; he'd said this a thousand times before. "Once through the last gate you'll be in forward territory, at the foot of the S-Bahn embankment. Wait ten minutes, then follow the border south for two hundred metres. After a down train has passed you have seven minutes before the next timetabled train is due. Climb the embankment, cross the down tracks and follow them to the end of the platform. Make sure no passengers see you in the track bed. When the next train arrives, leave the station with the other passengers. Any questions?"

★

The scout had made it all sound straightforward, but the actual act of passing through the gates and into the security strip felt disobedient. I looked around as the Border Scout carefully unclipped the signal wires on the gate through the fence, the floodlights had been turned off, but ambient light washed over the walls from the two Berlins lying either side of this thin line that divided East from West.

Before the final gate—a locked slab of concrete that hinged open at the base of the last wall—I changed out of my fatigues and into the black cord trousers and waistcoat of a working carpenter. With a deep breath, I stepped through the low opening and into no man's land.

I turned to the south, the Wall on my left: smooth concrete, over three metres tall, topped by a wide tube. Its presence felt familiar, it was the same design as the stretch of *Hinterland* wall near Ostbahnhof, along Stralauer Allee, a part of Berlin I regularly pass through. Except now I was on the other side.

I followed the foot of the embankment, counting my steps as I went. It was rough going, I couldn't see much and the bright lights from the station above prevented my eyes from getting used to the dark. I stumbled along like the village drunk making his way home from the pub after the street lamps have been turned off.

Once I'd nearly reached my destination, just twenty metres away from the platform, I pulled myself up the embankment, staying low, belly brushing over weeds. Near the top, I lay in the dusty undergrowth, waiting for the next down train to pass. It whined into the station, doors hissed open and the passengers who alighted moved down the platform. The platform manager shouted his command to stay back and the bell rang. Twenty seconds later, the S-Bahn rattled past, its wheels just a couple of metres from my head. The passengers could be seen behind lit windows, reading newspapers, dozing, chatting. None of them looked in my direction, nobody looked over the Wall. For them, the world ended at the side of the tracks.

The station was quiet, platforms swept empty by the chill wind. I checked the track was clear and crossed at an angle, giving the electrified third rail a wide berth.

The platform attendant looked away as I mounted the platform. I stayed at the end, behind the waiting room, out of sight of most of the platform.

The next train drew in and I walked alongside the train, as if to enter a carriage further along, but gradually changed direction to merge with passengers leaving the station. The crowd bunched up at the top of the steps to the street and I became aware of the aroma of the people around me. Perfume, deodorant, new clothes. I resisted the urge to stick my nose under my armpit, suddenly paranoid that people would smell my difference. Hard soap, disinfectant, brown coal, that's what they say we Easterners stink of.

It was in the middle of these paranoid thoughts that I spotted the cop.

He was standing in the roadway outside the station, watching us filter through the door. On the other side of the street was a VW Polo in green and white livery, a second cop sitting behind the wheel. He held a radio microphone and was talking into it, looking my way.

Sandwiched in the doorway, I was unable to move any way but forwards, passengers behind me were pushing me onwards. I watched as the first cop looked over his shoulder towards his colleague. He nodded, then with a glance back at the passengers, he returned to the car.

By the time I'd cleared the doorway, the cop was in the patrol car.

By the time I'd turned to go up the street, they'd gone.

By the next corner, my heart had slowed to its normal pace.

22
WEST BERLIN
Wedding

I followed my nose for a kilometre or so, past allotment gardens and heavy industry. I didn't need to bother with any stringent dry cleaning measures, there was so little traffic on the streets that anyone on my tail would have been obvious.

After a wide road, I entered a residential area. Tenement blocks were crammed together, paint flaked from window frames and the rendering was peeling off facades. Not so different from home.

The old buildings soon gave way to modern blocks of flats, the same kind of pre-fabricated slab-build that I live in. A yellow telephone booth stood at the next crossroads, I put three ten-Pfennig coins in and dialled the number the major had given me.

"Hilde Jahn speaking," a female voice, broken with age.

"This is Wilhelm, anything you want from the shops?"

"Please ask your sister to bring some flour. She's already there, in her red Golf. Speak to you tomorrow." Hilde put the phone down.

I found a newsagents and blinked as I stepped inside, thrown off-balance by the technicolour lurch of cultural jet-lag. From the bright shelves I selected a Falk map of Berlin and, once safely outside again, used it to trace my way to an underground station.

I got the U9 to the deep-south of West Berlin, then changed

to a bus that took me to Lichtenrade on the edge of the city. The bus dumped me more than a kilometre short of the border crossing used by the bin lorries and I walked towards it down Kirchhainer Damm—an extension of the same road that, on the other side of the border, I had travelled down many times.

It was a sleepy backwater of West Berlin, just dog walkers and office workers returning home after a hard day with the secretary. But every few minutes the neighbourhood was pulled back into the twentieth century by the passing of a heavy orange truck, shuddering past on its way to Schöneiche.

I was glad of the carpenter's wide-brimmed hat, tipping my head whenever a twenty-tonner went by, the better to hide my face from the drivers who weren't even looking my way.

The red Golf was parked on a strip of dirt between the road and a decaying woodland. Three hundred metres further on, I could see the hut used by the West Berlin police and customs officials who monitor the lorries using the crossing point.

I opened the door and got into the passenger seat without invitation, but the woman behind the steering wheel was expecting me. She kept her eyes on the checkpoint ahead, watching each truck as it came through, making a note of each and every registration plate.

"Hilde says she wants some flour," I told her.

Her eyes flickered in my direction. Hazel, flecked with orange that matched her copper hair. If I wasn't such an old cynic I could have fallen in love on the spot. But there's little that moves me now and I managed to remain professional.

"Hilde needs to find an outlet for her dramatic side," she observed. Her voice didn't match her eyes. It was hard, scratched with tobacco.

"I'm Wilhelm," I told her, but she didn't answer, her attention was on a truck that was passing the customs post.

"Time to find a new spot to park," she replied.

All work, this unnamed lady.

23
WEST BERLIN
Lichtenrade

The redhead started the engine and we did a U-turn. Three hundred metres further on, she pulled up outside a restaurant. It was a straight road, no turn-offs. We wouldn't miss any of the trucks coming from the border.

We sat in silence for the rest of the evening, moving the car every half an hour or so. Redhead had less to say for herself than old Harry and I wasn't in the mood to make an effort. She hadn't even given me a name yet, but if she wanted to be called *hey* or *you* then that was up to her.

At about ten o'clock it started raining. We cracked the windows open to stop the windscreen fogging up and my partner switched the wipers on every so often.

It was dark. I was cold, bored and uncomfortable.

I checked my watch, hoping it would be 11 o'clock already so we could end this joke of an observation. When finally the little hand had edged around that far, the woman either didn't notice or was enjoying my company so much she didn't want to leave.

"It's 2300 hours," I pointed out, ever so politely.

"Another ten minutes, in case the last one is late."

Ten minutes creaked by, punctuated every minute by a quick wipe of the windscreen.

Finally, she turned the ignition key.

★

We went back to her place, crossing most of West Berlin before ending up in Wedding, not far from Leopoldplatz, close to where I'd come across the border.

Redhead lived in a concrete flat, only the bright colour of the paint hiding behind even brighter graffiti marked this place as being in the West.

"Fourth floor," she told me as she let me in the front door.

I followed her up the four storeys and into her flat. It was as bare as a conspirational flat kept by the Firm.

While my contact was in the bathroom I had a quick look around her bedroom. Divan bed and mattress. Thin duvet in white cover. A glass of water and a wind-up alarm clock standing on the floor next to the bed.

That was it: nothing else.

A moment later, the bathroom was vacated and I made use of it. Shower gel, a bar of soap and a pink, disposable razor sat at the side of the sink. A cosmetic bag held foundation, blusher, lipstick in several shades, eyeliner and eyeshadow.

A red wig sat on top of the washing machine.

I came out of the bathroom with the intention of interrogating her, but she'd already gone into her bedroom and shut the door. A blanket was folded on the couch in the open plan kitchen-living room.

It looked like a piece of modern art. The concept stuff I'd seen in Western magazines confiscated at the border. But I'd seen this still life before.

Before making myself comfortable on the sofa, I checked out the kitchen area. There were no personal touches, this woman was either an ascetic or didn't live here.

The lack of food in the fridge confirmed my thoughts, but I was pleased by the pleasant selection of beer. I cracked open a bottle and opened up my notebook.

While I was in the operational area I wasn't to write any reports, but nevertheless, scrupulous accounting of my expenditure of hard currency was expected.

2,70 DM for my local transport ticket, 7,95 DM for the map. A bottle of water and a *Bild* newspaper for cover. Total: 11,60 in Westmarks.

Satisfied the bean counters back home wouldn't find anything to quibble over, I sat back and enjoyed a second beer.

My contact woke me at half-past four the next morning.

"Time to go," she told me.

"The hell it is," I told her. "You go if you want. Oskar only turns up at shift change—I'll join you in eight hours."

"You're on your own today." This morning she was a brunette. She was clearing away my beer bottles and emptying the ashtray. "I'm going to work."

Turns out my contact isn't a full-timer. Or if she is, she has a day job as part of her cover. Before she left, she handed me the keys to an Opel, along with instructions on where to find it.

When the door shut behind her, I got up for a piss then took another beer out of the fridge.

24
WEST BERLIN
Lichtenrade

I found the green Opel Kadett and drove down to Lichtenrade, positioning myself a couple of hundred yards from the border, same spot where I'd found my contact yesterday.

I had a clear view of the steel gates at the border, but couldn't see the checkpoint—that was hidden on the other side of a low hump that the road crossed as it went through the security strip.

The lorries arrived at the border with a rhythm as fast as a Young Pioneer marching song. They often jammed up on the access road, queuing back into West Berlin as the border guards checked documentation.

Coming back, they entered West Berlin more regularly, the border checks spacing them out evenly in two or three minute intervals.

At 1307 the lorry used by Oskar left West Berlin. I couldn't see the driver since I was facing the border crossing, but I picked up on his number plate. I started up the Kadett and drove back up the road to a yellow telephone box about a kilometre back. I had three Groschen coins ready and fed them in.

"Oskar has just gone shopping," I told the anonymous voice at the other end. It was Hilde. Maybe it was a different Hilde from yesterday, but it was still Hilde.

"Thanks for letting me know, Wilhelm." Hilde hung up, I

returned to my spot near the border.

This time I parked the other way round, all the better to pick up Oskar's tail when he came back from his trip to Schöneiche.

Watching the plates, I could tell the lorries were making the return trip to Schöneiche in eighty to a hundred minutes, but, true to form, Oskar didn't return until 1515—more than two hours after he'd crossed the border. When he went past, he was going at a fair pace, not dawdling as he had when I'd followed him the other night.

I fell in behind him, following the truck north to Tempelhof, where he got on the Stadtring motorway, heading west.

Traffic was light and he stayed in the right-hand lane most of the way, only overtaking an old Deutrans Volvo artic on the way. That meant I had to hang back a fair distance, but so far, all as expected: exit at Westend, main road to the waste incinerator in Ruhleben.

I watched him drive onto the site, but there was nowhere suitable for stationary observation so I carried on and pulled in at the sewage plant next door. A quick look at my map confirmed what I was thinking—there were only two ways out of this part of town: west to Spandau or east to the rest of Berlin.

No need to toss a coin: only thing that ever happened in Spandau was the changing of Rudolf Hess's prison guards.

I drove back a short way, finding a spot outside the gates of an allotment garden colony and waited for Oskar to emerge. This time I parked facing the direction he'd come from, all the better to make a positive identification.

Ten minutes later, a burgundy Ford Taunus exited the waste incinerator site and turned my way. Through the windscreen I could see a full head of curly, grey hair.

My man was on the move.

I went up the road and turned to come after Oskar. Tailing him was so easy it was boring. He took me down to Zoo

Station, past the Hollow Tooth—all the sights of West Berlin—but I had eyes only for his dark red Ford. We did a little right and left and ended up alongside the disused elevated railway and the fleamarkets in its stations. Another right-left wiggle and we were on Yorckstrasse, going under the derelict railway bridges and entering Kreuzberg. Over the busy Mehringdamm and turn a few corners.

We were now in a purely residential area, a block in from Gneisenaustrasse. The street was cobbled, plenty of potholes and the houses were in poor shape. A party of punks brayed on one corner, bottles of beer in hand. Turks wearing heavy moustaches and leather flat-caps brushed past them, ignoring the punks and ignored in turn.

But I was paying too much attention to the street life, when I looked forward again, Oskar's car had vanished. I cruised along, thinking he'd turned a corner into the next street, but there he was, just parking up.

I spotted him getting out of his Ford and eased further along the road until I found the right spot and pulled in, keeping one eye on my mirror the whole time.

I watched him push open the heavy carriage door to a tenement block and disappear from view.

After a minute or two, I checked the building. There were no doorbell buttons, but the street door wasn't locked. I shoved it open onto a dark passage, green gloss paint, dark with grime. The redness of an illuminated light switch glimmered in the dusk, so I pushed it. The lights thought about it for a moment before giving in and flickering into life.

It's no fun hiking up five storeys, checking names scrawled on scraps of cardboard glued below and beside doorbells. Most were illegible, faded to ghosts or unpronounceable combinations of letters. But there were no Schrabers or anything that was the right length or had any of the right letters.

Back down the steps and out into the back yard. A row of

galvanised steel bins on wheels were overflowing with brown coal ash, batteries, broken toys and food waste. On the other side of the yard was a side wing, a narrow door leading to even narrower stairs.

On the third landing I found Schraber.

Pressing an ear to the door, I could hear a TV. From the overwrought music and the shrill voices I guessed he was watching a soap opera. There were no other exits from the yard so, happy that I'd housed my man, I went back out to my car.

The punks had moved on and the Turks, seeing everything, seemed inclined to notice nothing. Nobody would bother me here.

25
WEST BERLIN
Kreuzberg

At this time of year it gets dark early. I sat in the Opel and watched sparks flicker from one street lamp to the next, running down the road like fuse wire, little explosions igniting the gas lights one after the other. Their buttery glimmer enabled navigation around the personnel mines left by dog walkers but was dull enough to allow strangers in parked cars to remain in the shadows.

Oskar exited his building at 2117, got into his Ford and headed west, returning the way we'd come a few hours earlier.

This time he didn't take us all the way to City West, he turned off onto Kurfürstenstrasse. A few bright shop windows zebra-ed the pavements with their reflections and girls with high heels and long legs prowled the kerb.

Oskar slowed down to view the goods and I pulled in to watch him make his selection.

A short thing in an even shorter dress was manoeuvring her cleavage into his line of sight when a sharp rap on the side window broke my concentration. It was a policeman's knock— the kind practised the world over on front doors at four in the morning and, here in West Berlin, on car windows at half-past nine in the evening.

"Driver's licence and vehicle registration documents," demanded the cop once I'd rolled down the window.

The first thing I needed to know was why he was hassling

me. A quick look around and I relaxed a little—a second squad car was parked further down the road, officers were checking other drivers, too.

Oskar had caught on to what was happening and was driving off, leaving his jail-bait by the side of the road. She joined the other prostitutes who were hurling the evil eye at the cops.

"I won't ask again: licence and registration documents." The bull's voice was as chilly as the night.

I pulled open the glove compartment, wondering what I'd find in there, but the shelf was as empty my contact's flat.

"*Donnerwetter,*" I swore quaintly. "My pal said he'd put the papers in here. I'm sorry officer ..."

He took my fake driver's licence, unfolding it and holding a torch close. It looked genuine enough, even to a cop, and I could recite the legend that was printed on it: Thomas Hasching, resident Heidelberg etc etc.

"Being in control of a vehicle without having the necessary papers is a misdemeanour, Herr Hasching," the cop lectured.

I did my best to look contrite, but he was already writing out the ticket. "Owner of the vehicle?"

"Walter Momper." I gave the bull the address of the up and coming West Berlin SPD politician and held my breath. If the cop called it in, he'd know within a couple of minutes that I was telling porkies.

While the cop put the finishing touches to his homework and decided what to do, I had another look around. Oskar's Ford was long gone.

"Right, get going," said the cop.

I held my hand out for the ticket, my forged licence and a lecture on documentation.

I put the Opel into gear, pulled out into the traffic, screwing the penalty notice up and chucking it out of the window as I went.

★

There was nothing to do but head back to Oskar's and hope to catch up with him there. On the way, I stopped off at a phone box and called my contact, telling her to meet me on Riemannstrasse.

Back in Kreuzberg, I found a good parking spot, went into the back yard and looked up at the dark windows of Oskar's flat. Wherever he was, he wasn't there.

Back at the car, I settled myself in for a long wait. I wasn't really asleep when my contact got into the car, but I wasn't fully awake either.

"What's the score," she asked.

So I told her the score, and that she might have to look for a new vehicle. I'd been expecting a tantrum, but now she was sitting in the car next to me I realised I'd be lucky to get any reaction at all.

"We'll get new registration plates," she told me. We sat there for a few minutes, watching Oskar's empty doorway.

"What are you called?" I was the first to cave in.

"Why?"

"I have to call you something, even if it's just something in my head. Even if it's *Tante* Gertrud." She smiled at that. It was the first time I'd seen any kind of expression on her mug. Progress. "What's so funny?"

"I had an aunt called Gertrud, that's all."

I wasn't sure whether to believe her. "Is that what we call you, then?"

"If you like."

We could have sat there all night, avoiding small talk, but I was ready for bed.

"Relieve me at five tomorrow morning," she said. "And phone Hilde, she'll send some new plates over. Tell her you've lost your shopping list, the one with the green cabbage on it."

"Vegetable shopping list? Seriously?"

But Gertrud was always serious.

26
WEST BERLIN
Wedding

I set Gertrud's alarm clock for four o'clock and rolled myself up in the blanket. Five hours later, I rolled off the sofa, splashed some water on my face and rubbed a hand over the stubble on my chin.

A few minutes after that I was standing in front of the Kadett, admiring the new plates. They weren't shiny new, they were dirty, the front one had a dint in it. I wondered whether there was another green Kadett pootling around Berlin with this same registration number.

At ten to five I was sitting next to Gertrud on Riemannstrasse.

"Arrived home 2243. I checked the lights in his flat at 2315 and again at 2330 by which time he'd gone to bed." Gertrud reported.

She left me her prime observation spot and I nudged the Opel alongside the kerb and watched her drive off in her red Polo.

An hour later, Oskar shouldered his way through the wide door of his tenement and stumbled across the road to his car. Compared to how he looked, I was Snow White: fresh and beautiful as a daisy.

I moved into the traffic behind him as he steered the car to Gneisenaustrasse, then another left as he turned onto Mehringdamm. We went past the airport buildings at

Tempelhof, heavy with masonry and history, but Oskar didn't turn off. I began to wonder whether he was heading for the border, whether he'd forgotten to pick up his orange truck, but he hung a right when we got to Alt-Mariendorf and pulled into the Kaisers central warehouse near the gasworks. I parked up and hunkered down in my seat.

I was too exposed here, but on the plus side, I could see what Oskar was up to. He parked his car and went into an office, through the open door I could see him take a card and punch in, returning the card to a rack on the wall.

After that I lost sight of him as he went further into the building, but I was satisfied. I had new information, even if I didn't know how or where to fit it in.

Ten minutes later, Oskar drove out of the car park—this time in charge of a red and white seven and a half tonne lorry with a smirking coffee pot on the side. Today, he was doing deliveries for a supermarket chain.

I let him get around the corner before starting the car up and going after him. He took me further west, into Zehlendorf and Dahlem, where the bosses live and the students trudge their way from the U-Bahn station to the Free University.

He made deliveries to a couple of small supermarkets, pushing roll pallets around his truck and giving them a ride on the tail lift.

Fun as all this was, I had other things to do. I left him while he was heading off to his next delivery and returned to the warehouse in Mariendorf.

The gates were open, only the small car park lay between me and the door to the offices. As I left the Opel I congratulated myself on today's attire—with my blue worker's overalls I should fit right in.

Pulling my cap down so the peak shaded my eyes and picking up a toolbox, I walked through the car park and up the steps. There was no watchman, nobody was interested enough to challenge me.

Just inside the door was the time clock, punch cards ordered alphabetically in a rack to the side. I scanned down to S, there he was: Schraber, Olli. I took his card out and laid it on top of the clock while I took a photo with a K16 pocket camera.

Back in the Kadett, I headed west again. I'd noticed a hospital this morning and I parked there now. Wherever there's a hospital, there's a phone box and once again, it was time to say hello to Hilde.

"It's Wilhelm," I said into the receiver.

"Good morning, Wilhelm. Aunty requests you come by for a visit."

"Understood."

That was my recall notice. Major Blecher was probably overreacting after my brush with the cops last night.

True, it was always best to avoid such encounters in the field and now I'd have to replace my legend. But I also knew that if I headed back over the Wall I probably wouldn't get a second chance to return, which meant I would never find out what Oskar was doing here in West Berlin.

Hospitals aren't just good for payphones, they're also good places to wait. You don't get noticed sitting in a car outside a hospital. And I had some sitting to do. And some thinking.

27
WEST BERLIN
Kreuzberg

The bar was called Malheur.

There was no sign of life to be seen from the outside, but once you'd pushed open the heavy door and climbed through the even heavier curtains, you knew this was the kind of pub that was always open.

I'd missed my appointment with the Wall, but I was where I wanted to be. The only thing I needed was alcohol.

The bartender was good. As I sat down on a stool, he was already topping up a tall glass. It was cold, it was beer. It was in front of me.

I signalled for another one and the young man on the other side of the bar nodded, respecting the silence of the transaction. He leant over, marked my beer mat with a soft pencil and started filling up a new glass.

I looked around. I didn't need to, there wasn't much to see and there wasn't much light to see it by.

But it felt like I was in the right place. The second beer arrived and I sat watching the bubbles rise, thinking my thoughts.

Since Hilde gave me the recall, I'd been back to Gertrud's sparse flat to pick up my bag. I left a note, telling her I'd gone home, that might confuse the trail a little if anyone thought of asking her.

I'd kept hold of the car, but I wouldn't be able to use it for much longer. Perhaps till midnight; any longer than that and I'd have either HA VIII or the boys from foreign intelligence, HV A, knocking on my windscreen, keen to take me home. If I could get new plates that might slow things down.

A job for later: cruise around West Berlin, looking for another green Kadett to swap with.

But that's not what I was thinking about as those bubbles swarmed up the side of my beer, popping on the golden surface and adding to the foam. I was thinking of Olli Schraber, codename Oskar.

Oskar the Kaiser's delivery truck driver.

Oskar the occasional driver of cross-border waste lorries.

Oskar the drunk.

28
WEST BERLIN
Kreuzberg

When Oskar walked in I wasn't surprised.

Relieved, yes, but not surprised.

I'd recognised something about him this morning, when he staggered out of his tenement and into his car. I'd recognised something about myself in him: Oskar was someone who preferred to spend his free time in a bar. And Malheur was his nearest pub.

I'd kept the seat next to me free, ignoring the reproachful looks of students and locals trying to find somewhere to sit. It was that kind of place, not a dark corner bar where you weren't allowed in unless you'd grown up and spent your whole life in the *Kiez*. Nor was it a cool place were students are efficiently stripped of their money. This was something in between, which made it a possible watering hole for Oskar.

If he hadn't turned up by 2200 hours, I would have risked the old-fashioned pub on the next corner, but I knew only a curtain of silence awaited me there.

When Oskar walked in, I pulled my bag off the seat next to me and hailed him.

"Jürgen!" I shouted joyfully at the door.

Oskar ignored me, heading for the tables at the back.

"Jürgen," I insisted as he went past.

He stopped for a moment, just long enough to mumble, *Wrong person*, something in that direction.

I didn't take the hint. "OK, not Jürgen," I conceded. "But you know me? Come on, two, maybe three years ago?"

Oskar was still hesitating, I had my foot in the door. "You're a driver. I do engines—you were having a bad day, I gave you a pull on my hip flask," I told him.

"Where?" Oskar was sceptical, but not nervous. He thought I had the wrong man but wasn't a hundred per cent sure—the hip flask story was believable.

"Olli! That's it—you're Olli." I gave him a relieved laugh, beckoned at the empty chair next to me.

Oskar didn't move, but he didn't look away either. He was examining my face, it might have looked familiar. He'd seen me once before, last week at Schöneiche, but at the time he hadn't been paying attention. Plus, I was now wearing three days of stubble and a pair of thick-rimmed glasses.

In any case, you see someone working on a landfill site in East Germany, the last place you expect them to jump out at you is in your local filling station in West Berlin—East German workers don't get to cross borders that easily.

"Couldn't tell you where it was, though," I said, keeping up the patter. "I work all over, day here, day there. Höffner, Zapf removals—did a stint at Kaisers ..." Oskar's face lightened, I pushed my advantage. "Listen, I'll get you a beer—I owe you one. You gave me some good advice that time, never forgotten it." I was already signalling to the bar staff, two beers.

Seeing that the beer was already on its way, Oskar settled in the chair next to me.

"What was the advice I gave you," he asked, still trying to place me.

"My wife. I was having problems with her, you know? But you put me straight."

"Told you to leave her, did I?" Oskar was half-serious, prepared to smile if the joke went the right way.

"Exactly!" I clapped him on the shoulder. "Sound advice, that was."

The beers arrived and we clinked glasses. Oskar still didn't know who I was, but he was prepared to give me the benefit of the doubt for the sake of the free beer.

"You still at Kaisers?" I asked him.

"Yeah. Deliveries. Pays the bills, y'know?"

"They still using those MAN seven-halfers?"

"Them's the ones." Oskar snorted another mouthful of beer. He checked his pockets for a cigarette pack, but I already had some in my hand. Lucky Strike, the brand Oskar liked to smoke. He fed the nail in and got it lit.

He was where I wanted him, most of the way down his first beer and feeling comfortable with it. We talked diesel engines and gearboxes for a while. I could remember enough from my military service days to bluff along and Oskar was happy to be in the driving seat of the conversation.

Two beers later he was mellow and we were old pals.

"What you doing here?" he waved his empty glass at the pub at large.

"Long story. You probably haven't got the time." I pretended to hold back.

"What we're here for, isn't it? Beer and chat?"

"Living in Heidelberg now, came back here for a few days. A lady, if you know what I mean?" I caught his eye and nodded.

"Didn't go so well, then?"

"Why'd you say a thing like that?" I overplayed mock-offence, let him know I was happy to joke about it.

"If it were going well you wouldn't be here drinking beer with me, would you?"

"Impeccable logic, my friend! Can't fault it." I nodded sadly.

"So what's the score, then?"

"Met this lady in Heidelberg. She's from Berlin, heard my accent, knew I was from her neck of the woods. Long story short, we got chatting. Next thing is, she's inviting me to come and visit. I couldn't wait, know what I mean? Worst thing I ever did, leave Berlin."

Oskar nodded. We were in agreement on that score. Another round came in and we busied ourselves with taking the edge off the new beers.

"So," I continued. "I get off the train at Zoo—all that hassle with the border checks on the transit train, you know how it is—knackered by the time I got here. Off the train, straight on the U-Bahn and over to her flat." I checked I still had my audience. Other than the beer I was benefiting from all his concentration. "Nobody home. So I hang about a bit, you know, thinking she's just popped out to run some messages. Next thing I know, this old biddy turns up, wanting to know what I'm doing sitting outside her flat." Oskar laughed as I mimed being hit with a handbag. "Right *Rabatz*, it was."

"So what happened to your woman?" he wanted to know.

"Dunno. Came straight here."

"Did the right thing, mate."

"Got my return ticket back to Heidelberg, there's an express leaves just before eleven, gets me home in time for breakfast. I'll have to get that."

Oskar clinked glasses in commiseration.

"Shame, would have liked to see if I could find her. You know, might have got the wrong address, something like that."

"Why don't you do that?" Oskar was drunk enough to have to emphasise each word. It was going well.

"Haven't got anywhere to kip, mate." I checked my watch. "Listen, I'll get the next round in, then I'll have to head off."

Dismayed at the possibility of having to pay for the rest of the night's beers, Oskar rose to the challenge: "But you've got to find her. Misunderstanding, that's what it is. Stay at mine if you like, you'll find her tomorrow."

I got another round in to celebrate.

29
WEST BERLIN
Kreuzberg

Oskar chucked me out just before six o'clock. He was still bleary from the beer but capable of speech.

"Good luck finding your woman," he told me as he handed over a slip of paper with his phone number. "Give me a call next time you're in Berlin, we'll go for a drink."

We parted on Riemannstrasse. He went off to work, I went off to find the green Opel. I'd parked it in a street on the other side of Gneisenaustrasse, near the canal and the America Memorial Library.

It was close enough to walk, but not too close to make it easy to find me.

I strode along, head held high, satisfied with the night's work. Oskar had given me a tatty blanket and pointed to the couch, then passed out on his bed.

Once I was sure he was out for the count, I'd had a look round. If I'd been expecting fifty thousand Deutsche Marks in used notes I would have been disappointed, but I was after smaller game. I found two keys on a split ring in the drawer under the telephone, a key for a cylinder lock along with a heavy warded key.

I tried one key on the flat door and when it worked, went downstairs and tested the warded key on the front door to the street. It did the job. Both keys went into my pocket.

Other than that, there was little to see. Oskar's flat was

comfortable but didn't feel lived in. That's not to say it was tidy, far from it, but, as I'd guessed, he preferred to spend his free time down at the bar and it showed.

This morning, as I got to the end of Zossener Strasse and turned right before the canal, I held the spare keys to Oskar's flat in my pocket. If I'd had my kit with me I could have put a bug in his phone there and then. As it was I'd have to make contact with Hilde, see if she could supply. Might be a bit awkward, seeing as I'd been expected in the East some nine hours ago.

The car was in sight now and I was getting my keys out when the bag went over my head.

I twisted to my right and used my elbow to try to catch whoever was behind me, but without being able to see there was no way to aim. A hard stamp down in the hope of catching a foot, but I caught only the pavement.

My arms were pulled behind my back. I knew what was coming next, but it didn't help. The fist met my left kidney and I doubled over. As my head went down, the hands behind me pushed me into the boot of a car.

The lid slammed shut and I was a prisoner.

30
UNKNOWN

Each noise, each bump, each change of speed and direction take on new significance when you're tied up in the trunk of a car. Each halt at a junction and each turn of a corner gives you a fresh bruise. I tried to make sense of the route we were taking, but my sense of geography in West Berlin wasn't good enough.

Was I being taken through the Wall, back home to the East? Or was I in the hands of the local *Verfassungsschutz*, the West Berlin security agency? Each of the Western Allies also got a mention in my mental list, but the truth was, I didn't know who had me.

Whoever it was, they had been professional about it. I'd seen neither them nor the car I was bundled into, not that the make and model or the registration plates of a vehicle would be reliable indicators.

Right now, I wasn't even sure who I wanted my captors to be. If it was the home team, they'd probably send me back to Hohenschönhausen prison and that would be no fun. If it was a Western agency then I simply didn't know how they'd treat me—but I'd have no choice but to find out.

Whichever way you looked at it, things could be better.

I closed my eyes when they pulled the hood off my head. Not much light made it inside whatever building we were in, but it was still much brighter than inside that bag.

As my eyes adjusted, I could see we were in a small garage,

three men on one side, a Mercedes saloon on the other, boot yawning open.

"March," one of the thugs ordered me. He spoke German with a Saxon accent. But even before he'd opened his gob I had them pegged as being from the Firm.

I was among friends. But were they friendly?

They shoved me through a side door and as we walked out into daylight, I had to blink again, even though it was a dull October day and we were in a dull new-build project. Ten-storey flats, one after another, making a giant's courtyard.

Obviously I couldn't see beyond the high buildings surrounding me, but I had the feeling that next to this square there'd be another, identical one, and one after that. If my feeling was right then we were in Marzahn.

One of the goons shoved me up the steps to a door and we all had fun standing too close together in the undersized lift. We ratcheted up the inside of the building until the doors dragged themselves open to reveal a terrazzo-lined hall.

One of the flat doors stood open and I was pushed inside. My wrists were untied by a goon and I was allowed to shake my arms to let the blood know it was time to reacquaint itself with hands and fingers.

While my fingers tingled, a shove in the back told me to use the door ahead. I tried the handle and went in, shutting the door behind me.

"Surprised to see me, Reim?" It was Major Blecher. He wasn't in a polite mood.

"Not surprised to see you, Comrade Major, more surprised to be here at all," I answered.

Blecher had made himself comfortable in an armchair. I made myself comfortable leaning against the wall. I won't pretend I wasn't worried, but sometimes it's best not to let it show too much.

"Cigarette?" He gestured to an ashtray and a deck sitting on the wall unit.

Condemned men are entitled to a last smoke so I fed myself a nail—fancy brand it was, Club—and went back to my piece of wall, watching the major through the haze rising from the tip. It was all a bit confusing.

"You've got one chance," the major informed me. "Don't waste it."

I didn't need more than one chance to explain myself—there was only one story to tell: I disobeyed a recall because I had a hunch I could crack Oskar. I took the cigarette out of my mouth, about to tell the major what he wanted to know, but then I had a thought.

I put the nicotine-rod back where it belonged and while I was puffing away, I considered what my brain was trying to tell me. It was all very simple—the major was just as confused as I was.

If he'd been sure of his ground, I'd already be down in the cellars of Hohenschönhausen. So why wasn't I?

We watched each other across the room. I could hear the thoughts turning over in my head, they sounded like a Trabant engine drinking from a batch of bad petrol.

Major Blecher's left eyelid was quivering. He was worried I was working for more than one side.

He didn't want to share this operation with HA I, we'd established that already. And I was working unofficially on the major's orders while my superior officer thought I was tucked away in Schöneiche, watching Western rubbish being tipped on East German land.

And now I thought of it, I still wanted to know about the major's reasons for setting me on to Oskar, first in Schöneiche, then in West Berlin. At first, I'd been happy to get away from work on the landfill. Now I'd got involved, I also wanted to know what Oskar was up to. But, more than that, finding out what the major's interest was might give me an advantage when everything started flying around our ears.

If I got through this I'd have a stiff word with myself, tell myself to pay more attention in future. I caught that thought before it wandered off down familiar paths and pulled my focus back. The major was still sitting there, impatient eyes upon me.

Buy some time, I told myself.

I bounced myself off the wall and stood up straight. "Comrade Major, I have made contact with subject Oskar, including entering his dwelling." I avoided the question of my being absent without leave and focussed on the case.

When the major didn't react in any meaningful way I took Oskar's keys out of my pocket and stepped forward to lay them on the table by the major's chair. "I suggest amending the operational plan to allow operational control of the subject in addition to the current measures of passive observation."

There was silence while Major Blecher stared at the keys.

"You've already engaged in operational control measures," he observed mildly. He was right. I'd gone well beyond the observational role I'd been briefed for, but I was happy to let him decide whether I had done so on my own initiative or under the instructions of a different department.

"Does anyone else have copies of those keys?" He asked finally.

"No, Comrade Major."

He cheered up when he heard that. Another pause for thought, then came the question I'd been hoping for.

"Why don't you sit down, Comrade Second Lieutenant Reim, we can discuss our next steps."

31
BERLIN MARZAHN

Before we started talking operational schnick-schnack, the major decided we should have a coffee.

I listened with half an ear as he talked to the goons in the hall—I was keen to get advance notice if he was about to order them to arrest me. As it was, he just dismissed them.

Relieved, I got back to exercising my brain while the major sorted through kitchen cabinets looking for coffee. There were plenty of other departments at the Ministry who would be interested in Oskar, providing of course that they found out about his activities. My own department, responsible for Westerners who had entered the GDR would have a legitimate interest, as would Schalk-Golodkowski's boys in KoKo—they were the ones who had brokered the waste disposal deal with West Berlin and who ran the tip. And they were the ones who'd end up with red faces if it got out that one of the West Berlin drivers might be up to no good.

Then there was HA II, counter-intelligence, and HV A, foreign intelligence who'd get mightily excited if they caught wind of this operation.

And the Simson motorbike registered to the local border regiment opened up the case for interest by yet another department: HA I, responsible for observing the armed forces.

So, I reasoned, it wasn't so surprising if the major should wonder whether I'd been approached by another department. Let's face it, if another section of the MfS wanted to enlist me, they wouldn't give me the option of saying no. In return, I would be entitled to a certain level of protection should the major take against me.

So it was in my interests to allow the major to believe I was involved with another department. The other option, admitting to directly disobeying an order, would see me back behind bars before the coffee had cooled.

The major came back into the room and we skirted around the issue of departmental responsibility like a couple of virgins.

Instead, we talked about my assessment of Subject Oskar. I wasn't the only one in this room trying to buy some time while he worked out what to do. The major suggested kitting me out with the necessary hardware and sending me back into West Berlin to install surveillance equipment in Oskar's flat. My crossing would be scheduled for after darkness, leaving me at a loose end for the rest of the day.

"We can't have operatives crossing the security strip in daylight," he told me.

"Could I use another conspirational crossing?"

The major looked uncomfortable. We were both familiar with the situation at Friedrichstrasse station. An inconspicuous door in an underground interchange, never noticed by the commuters who used the corridor to cross between the West S-Bahn and the West U-Bahn, all beneath the streets of East Berlin.

"Other possibilities would require the co-operation of the relevant departments," he admitted.

There it was, out in the open. The major wasn't keen to trust any of the other departments that made up the Firm.

Which just made me wonder all the more.

32
BERLIN PANKOW

"Wait until a down train passes. You have seven minutes to cross the tracks and get on the platform before the next train is due ..." The lanky sergeant was giving me the same spiel as last time. He wasn't paid to notice who had been through before, in fact, he was paid not to notice his clients. "When the next train arrives, leave the station with the other passengers. Any questions?"

I had no questions.

The major and I had cleared the air, at least as much as could be expected under the circumstances, so now I was on my way back to the West, suited and booted in army fatigues, my Puma bag back in its green duffel disguise.

I changed into my *Westler* clothes in the shadow of the last gate, where there was a deliberate flaw in the coverage of the floodlighting. The sergeant took my army togs, opened up the hinged concrete flap at the bottom of the wall and I limboed through into forward territory.

I made the platform without anyone seeing me, blended with the passengers leaving the next train. Same procedure as last time. Every detail, right down to the cop waiting outside the station, his colleague in a patrol car on the other side of the street. It was a different policeman, but he scanned the exiting passengers in the way all policemen do.

This time, I went with the crowds, carried along to the bus stop at the end of this part of Wollankstrasse. Behind us, the closed off arches of the railway bridge blocked the way to

Wollankstrasse in the East, down which I'd been driven in a Border Troops truck not half an hour since.

Half an hour of changing clothes, passing through gateways, past signal fences and Czech-hedgehogs, all to arrive a hundred yards from my starting point.

The bus arrived and I got on, stamping my ticket in the machine and sitting down.

Seven stops later, I alighted.

If I turned left and walked a few hundred meters, I'd reach the border crossing point Chausseestrasse and be halfway home. But I turned right, heading towards Leopoldplatz, the heart of Berlin-Wedding.

Leopoldplatz itself is more than just a square. It's the nearest bit of open space for the hemmed-in residents of this quarter. As I crossed the square I moved through layers of Wedding society: more Turks, fewer students and punks than in Kreuzberg. Round here, the spaces between the Turks were filled by proletarian workers sitting on benches and drinking beer.

A couple of streets later I was at Gertrud's flat. I let myself in, the place was empty. Her cosmetics bag and wigs were gone, the bed was stripped. But the fridge was still full of beer. This was my kind of safe flat.

33
WEST BERLIN
Kreuzberg

The next morning I sat in my puke-green Opel Kadett outside Codename Oskar's tenement, waiting for him to make a move.

He appeared on time, loping down the road, trying to remember where he'd parked his car. I sat back and waited for him to sort himself out, then nudged the Opel out of the parking space and followed Oskar down to his workplace in Mariendorf.

Once I'd seen him onto a delivery lorry, I turned round and headed back to Kreuzberg.

Oskar's telephone was a standard, dark green Bundespost job. The one with the black push buttons.

I lifted the receiver and checked the dial tone. That was the easy bit done.

Letting myself out of his flat, I headed downstairs to the cellars. Rough wooden palisades divided off each flat's storage space, the gates secured by an assortment of padlocks, each of which could have been picked by a Young Pioneer armed with nothing more than a fork from the school canteen.

But my attention was on the ceiling—flaked whitewash hung like bat wings and a slew of dark cables ran along one edge. The wires disappeared into a black plastic box marked POST and that's where I started the job.

The main telephone cable into the building divided into

several rows of terminal blocks. I disconnected the fourth set of red and black cables, then went upstairs to check Oskar's phone. The phone was dead, I had the right connection. Back in the cellar, I connected Oskar's line to one pair of cables and attached another couple of wires to his terminals. I wound the new wires around the other telephone cables until they were near a likely looking storage compartment full of old boxes and broken toys dusty with neglect.

From a hidden corner, I swept up a small amount of dust from the top of an old sewing machine bench, then pushed a cardboard box to one side, making space behind it, near to an electrical plug. From my bag I took a tape recorder, set it up next to the plug and fed both pairs of wires into a magic box, with another pair connected between that and a tape recorder.

Upstairs, the telephone's own microphone would pick up both sides of any telephone conversation and the box of tricks I'd just connected fed the pick-up to the sound activated tape recorder. I pushed the packing box back a bit to hide my kit, leaving enough space to reach in and change the cassettes, then gently blew the dust I'd collected over the floor and box where I'd disturbed the layer of dirt.

Satisfied with my work, I headed upstairs once more to check Oskar's telephone was working as well as could be expected.

The whole job had taken half an hour, I noticed as I let myself out of Oskar's tenement and walked up Riemannstrasse. That was a personal record.

34
WEST BERLIN
Kreuzberg

I found a quiet cafe on Mehringdamm and bought myself a coffee and a sandwich roll from the Anatolian waiter.

I wanted some space and time for myself, to catch up on the old thinking. Gertrud's empty flat would have done the job, but for the moment, I wanted to be somewhere I couldn't be found.

So far I'd spent over four Westmarks and had only the snack in front of me to show for it. I wasn't worried about the bean counters any more, I knew from Major Blecher's behaviour that minor infringements of operational regulations would no longer count. At the end of this operation I'd either get a medal and a promotion or I'd never see the light of day again.

The major and I had negotiated what Machiavelli would have been pleased to call a truce. We both wanted the same thing: to know who the other party was working for, and by extension, who they were working against.

Had the major realised I was a mere pawn in this game, I would have been out on my ear—I'd already shown myself to be untrustworthy, liable to ignore the operational plan whenever it suited me. That had got us results so far, but once you got to the pay grade where you were obliged to wear all that heavy braid on your shoulder boards, you tended to prefer obedience to initiative when it came to underlings.

In my mind, Operation Magpie and Subject Oskar were already fading into the background—mere context to the struggle for my own survival. Office politics had never been my strong point, but this time I had no choice but to play the major's game.

I had some ideas, and I mulled them over while I munched on my roll, rejecting one thought after another, almost with each swallow. The obvious course of action was to feed the major's suspicions—give him more reason to believe that I was working for another department. It would be easy to do—allow myself to be seen with officers from other parts of the Ministry, let the major catch sight of a mocked-up draft report addressed to KoKo. That kind of thing.

Too heavy-handed, and much too risky, I decided. If the major felt threatened then the plan could backfire, make him feel he had to cover himself by taking action against me. If that happened then the best I could hope for would be for him to quietly drop me. Then I'd end up back on the landfill in Schöneiche, spying on binmen and tip-workers until I retired.

No, I needed to remain indispensable, yet at the same time pose a threat. A minor threat, nothing too scary for the delicate major.

That's good, I like a challenge.

35
SCHÖNEICHE

"Decided to join us again?" The Brigade Leader had spotted my approach. He didn't sound particularly friendly.

"They might have to operate again," I told him.

He assessed my gait as I walked up to him. I had a small stone in my shoe to remind myself which leg to favour and I wasn't hamming my limp.

"All this because of a graze." The gaffer shook his head. He was trying to work out what to do with me.

The nice thing would have been to stick me in the gatehouse with my old pal, Harry. But I was needed on the bulldozer.

"Take the scraper," he told me. "See how you get on. If it doesn't work out we'll let you keep Harry company." He turned away and marched back to his armchair in the plant shed. All heart, our gaffer.

I got behind the levers of the Russian-built bulldozer and started her up. Black diesel exhaust smeared my rear windscreen until I was far enough up the bank of rubbish for the breeze to blow the smoke away. The first orange lorries were arriving with their West Berlin waste and a queue formed behind me as I tracked along the temporary roadway.

I got into position and started shovelling soil and household waste over steel barrels that were being tipped into a shallow pit.

It was good to be back.

★

I paid Harry a visit during my lunch break. He sat by the slidey window, knees pressed up against his oil heater under the desk.

"You here again?" he asked as I joined him at the window.

"Miss me?"

"They might have." Harry pointed out of the window, towards the plant shed, where some of the other workers were gathered around the gaffer's brazier.

"How'd it go?" asked the gaffer as I limped my way to the gate at shift-end. He was still interested in my leg, wondering whether I was malingering.

"Fine," I told him. "Not too bad at all."

I got a grunt for an answer. I schlepped through the gate and didn't turn around, even though I could feel his eyes on my back.

As soon as it was dark, I fired up the motorbike.

Patrol, the major had ordered. *Do a bit of patrolling, keep your eyes open for anything out of the ordinary.* That was the deal I'd made with him. I'd go back to Schöneiche, keep an eye on things; he'd let me know if anything useful came off the audio tapes from Oskar's flat.

An operative in West Berlin, perhaps Gertrud, would go to Oskar's cellar once a day to change the tapes and hand them over to a courier for analysis back at Berlin Centre. We were hoping we'd get a heads up on his next visit to Schöneiche.

Advance notice would mean that, for the first time ever, we could be in position to observe him on his first trip, not just on the second.

We didn't know whether the first delivery would be any different from the one he'd take a few days later, but there had to be a reason for the way he always came over the border twice in a few days then wasn't seen again for weeks or even months.

103

I rode from Mittenwalde to Grossmachnow, then down the F96 as far as Zossen. I turned around and came back the same way.

Anything out of the ordinary, I shouted into the headwind. The closer you got to Zossen, the less ordinary anything was. The biggest Russian camp outside the Soviet Union was just to the south of the town and huge areas of the forest around it were off-limits to us East Germans.

Round here it would be surprising if you saw anything ordinary.

36
BERLIN TREPTOW

The next Sunday, I headed back to Berlin to give my regular report to my immediate superior, Captain Funke.

I handed over the file that I'd typed up that morning in my office and he put it on top of a stack of other files on his desk. "Anything to report?"

"Nothing to report, Comrade Captain Funke."

Funke seemed to have lost interest in Operation Magpie, he dismissed me and got back to more important files.

I left the Clubhouse and pointed the MZ back towards Schöneiche. Somebody else might have been pissed off by Funke's indifference, but I recognised that if my superior officer no longer expected weekly reports and reassurances of steady progress then I'd have more freedom to follow Major Blecher's interests. And my own.

Once on the motorway, I opened the throttle, ignoring my exit at Mittenwalde and continuing on as far as Lübbenau, then taking small roads around the edges of the brown coal pits that puncture the landscape.

I stopped in a village with no name. Half derelict houses, grey with age, dusty with sand. But it had a pub, and the pub had food. A plate of pig's belly with sauerkraut and boiled potatoes, a glass or two of beer and it felt like Sunday again.

Back on the bike, I picked up the F96 at Finsterwalde and headed north. I got stuck behind a convoy of Soviet trucks, no way to overtake them, nothing to do but wind the throttle back and think pleasant thoughts.

Every case has a thread running through it—any and all loose ends tie into that central thread sooner or later. My last case, the one that had landed me first in prison then in this plum job on the dump, the thread that time had been the Boss's fancy woman.

It's usually a person, someone who's done something, or had something done to them. But this time, it felt like the connecting thread was a road, the very road I was dawdling along right now.

It was the same road the West Berlin bin lorries came down to dump their unwanted waste on our land. It was the road that crossed into West Berlin via a checkpoint set up just for the waste transports. After the border, it threaded its way through West Berlin, past Oskar's day job at the Kaisers warehouse, past his flat in Kreuzberg before passing close to the safe flat in Wedding.

Right now though, I was far to the south, trapped behind this convoy. I could have turned off and found another route, but we were coming to the point where F96 diverted westwards. When the Russians took over half the town of Wünsdorf for their headquarters, they decided they didn't want civilians driving through the middle of it. At the crossroads at what used to be the centre of Wünsdorf, the convoy carried straight on, entering Little Russia. I did what the rest of the domestic traffic did and took the diversion.

What was Major Blecher's interest in the Russians? For him, it was all about Oskar and Russians. At every debrief he wanted to hear whether our Soviet friends had cropped up at all in my investigations. But so far all I had on them was the one incident on my second night here when I caught them disinterring old copies of Playboy at the tip.

According to old Harry the watchman, the West German driver Richard was involved in some trading with the Soviet soldiers, I could follow up on that angle.

I'd approach him again, see if I couldn't find anything out.

37
MICHENDORF

Richard Harm was a truck driver. Two to three times a week, always Monday and Wednesday, sometimes Friday, he'd make the journey from somewhere in Hessen in West Germany, up the motorway to Braunschweig and across the border and into the GDR at Marienborn.

He mostly carried special waste and if I was on the early shift I'd have the pleasure of his company. He'd raise the bed of his trailer, pour out the liquid or semi-liquid waste and I'd bulldoze some crap over the top.

At any time in the last few weeks, he could have got out of his cab and tried to sell me some Western goods. But he hadn't. Perhaps he'd decided, as rumour at the site had it, to concentrate on catering to the needs of the Russians.

Perhaps he just didn't like the look of me.

The next week I was on late shift, which meant that I wouldn't be working mornings when Richard made his deliveries.

I spent Monday morning at Michendorf service station, watching the traffic go by on the Autobahn. Michendorf is one of those places where domestic traffic and transit traffic between West Berlin and West Germany meet. East and West mix in the restaurant, local families and distant relatives from the West sit together and chat. That's one of the reasons the Firm keeps a sharp eye on the place.

I knew I'd be conspicuous, hanging around and observing traffic go by, so the first thing I did on arrival was make myself known to the watchers.

They appeared to accept my story at face value. They'd also log the event, probably check the registration of the Trabant I was in, but as long as they didn't interfere I didn't care what they did.

There was no need to wait long, Richard's white Magirus-Deutz throbbed past in the right-hand lane and I wound up my Trabant to go after him. Normally a Trabi and a fully-laden Western truck are about even in terms of speed, but I was in the car that Personal Protection had lent me and the fine-tuning they'd given the engine meant I that little bit extra under the hood.

Because of that, but also because I knew where Richard was heading, I was relaxed about keeping him just out of sight. I sped up every so often to check he was still on track, then let a few trucks and buses get between us again.

He came off at Rangsdorf, turning south onto the F96. From then on he was on the same route as the bin lorries from West Berlin.

I stayed on his tail as he rumbled through Rangsdorf and turned onto the local road at Grossmachnow. Richard was a careful driver, scrupulous about speed limits and every other traffic regulation. There was nothing interesting about the man, except for the rumours of his black market activities.

I followed him as far as the tip, then, not wanting to draw any attention to myself, drove back to my lodgings.

"Letter for you, Herr Linsner." The landlady was waiting for me in the hall.

I took the envelope upstairs before opening it. It was an appointment at the Friedrichshain hospital in Berlin for an operation on my leg. I was to report tomorrow morning, a sick note was enclosed.

That was my signal, Oskar had been activated. He would be delivering waste to Schöneiche tomorrow.

38
SCHÖNEICHE

I clocked off at the end of my shift, somehow managing to avoid the Brigade Leader. He'd already had a good moan at me when I gave him my sick note at the start of my shift and I didn't intend giving him another chance for a grumble.

From the landfill I went straight to the safe flat in Berlin-Pankow. The major was waiting for me when I let myself in. He was sitting in a dusty armchair, blanket over his legs and a flask of coffee by his hand. The iron stove was pumping out heat and a naked low-watt bulb burnt from the ceiling rose. Very cosy.

"Oskar received a phone call last night. He's to visit you tomorrow at the usual time," The major said.

I remained where I was, waiting for him to tell me if there was anything more.

"Do you have to clutter up the landscape?" he asked.

I found myself a chair in another room and carried it through to where Blecher was sitting. Wallpaper hung in strips from the damp walls, the plaster beneath was spongy and was making detailed plans for retreat.

"Next steps?" I asked. It wasn't the kind of place to stand to attention in. Neither of us were in uniform and the usual rules no longer seemed to apply anyway.

"Observation of subject, what else?" the major snapped, pouring coffee into the cup of the flask. He didn't offer me any.

"Do you want me in the operational area or on our side?"

The major didn't answer, he was too busy blowing the surface of his hot coffee. Steam rolled up and added to the general dampness.

Not to be outdone, I pulled out my hip flask. This was pushing it, perhaps too far, but it would be good to know how the major would react. A swig, screw the lid back on. I didn't offer the major any. He didn't react.

"Your thoughts?" the major asked. He had the patronising tone officers used when they didn't know what to do.

But I was prepared, I'd thought about this on the drive into Berlin and had my answer ready. West Berlin was where I'd find the next piece of the Oskar puzzle: I wanted to find out what Oskar picked up before he left the city on the way to Schöneiche, whether it was a package or a message.

"I want to be in West Berlin," I told the major. "Is Oskar already under surveillance in the operational area?"

The major shook his head.

"All the more reason for me to be over there. I'll brief the observation team on this side before I cross," I told him. There were things they needed to be aware of, like the stopping places and the tracks through the woods.

"Observation team?" Blecher looked up from his coffee. The steam must have irritated his eye, he rubbed it. "There is no observation team. It's just you, Comrade Second Lieutenant."

Perhaps it shouldn't have, but this surprised me. No team on standby, ready to watch Oskar's every move on either side of the border, just me over here and Gertrud in West Berlin.

Not the best way to run an operation.

I fetched a cigarette out and put it between my lips. The smoke curled up. It was finer than the steam from the major's coffee. More suited to augury, but I found no guidance in those tendrils of vapour and particulates.

"Comrade Major," I began, then stopped. I started again, this time more calmly, trying to crowbar a bit of respect into my tone. "Comrade Major, am I correct in observing that I am the

110

only one engaged in operational contact with Oskar?"

The major inclined his head. As good an acknowledgement as I was going to get.

A case like this should have three teams and round the clock eyes on the subject. If Gertrud and I were the only ones even allowed anywhere near Oskar and I was the only allowed to actually have contact with him, then the only plan that made sense was for Gertrud to tail him in West Berlin. I'd have to remain here and try to find out what he did in the small woodland between Mittenwalde and Grossmachnow.

39
GALLUN

I was still of the opinion that I could achieve more by observing Oskar in West Berlin. I could organise observation on this side of the border, which would free me up to head over the border. A few of the *Kripo* in Königs Wusterhausen had been helpful in the schlamassel that had been my previous case. Very capable, and discreet with it—the obvious candidates for a discreet job like this.

But that relied on the major's approval, and I already knew that wouldn't be forthcoming. Without his say-so I couldn't cross to West Berlin.

So I had to stay here, observe Oskar on his journey from the border crossing point to Schöneiche and back again.

My problem was that there were two distinct entry and exit points to the woods where Oskar put in a pit stop. Approaches from both ends of the road needed to be covered along with at least two pairs of eyes on the clearing.

And as I keep saying, I was on my own.

The next morning I decided to make an early start. I didn't know when Oskar's contact would turn up, and it was possible he might have the meeting place under surveillance.

That's why I was up three hours before the sun, pulling on my dash-no-dash fatigues and a fleece *Bärenvotze* hat. I checked the clip and chambered a round in my Walther PP. The pistol went in a shoulder holster under my jacket.

Parking the motorbike at the entrance to an allotment

colony the other side of Mittenwalde, I walked across the fields to the back of the woods halfway along the road to Grossmachnow. The moon was a fine sliver in the sky, shedding little light, barely enough to give me orientation. I kept one eye on the sky, the other on the road to my right.

The field was bare for the winter and provided no cover, so at any sign of movement I had to press my nose to the ploughed earth. That happened three times before I made the edge of the woods and was able to slip through the outer band of trees before lowering myself onto one knee. I stayed there for ten minutes, listening to the sounds around me. A deer stepped my way, finally noticing me when the breeze stirred and blew my scent around. The deer stopped, ears aloft, nosing trouble but not seeing any, before giddily dancing away, legs high and tail higher.

Once I had a feel for the woods, I used a compass to navigate on heading 50 mil until I was within sight of headlights going along the road. I hunkered down and waited for pre-dawn light.

When the Prussian blue of night lifted to the two-dimensional grey of first light I made my way towards the clearing. I stopped every few metres to observe and listen to my surroundings, alive to any movement. Seeing and hearing nothing, I pressed on until I reached the fallen log.

No fresh cigarette ends this time, no new litter. Nothing to indicate any recent visitors.

I moved away from the clearing in the opposite direction from the two paths. Fifty metres from the clearing and a few metres higher up the slope I found what I needed. A shallow depression behind a young oak still hanging on to its papery leaves. I had my position to observe Oskar from.

40
MITTENWALDE

The boredom isn't the worst thing, nor is the cold. Not being able to smoke for nine hours is a drag. Cramp can be warded off with minor movements, the flexing of toes and heels. The killer is always that you never know when or whether your patience will be rewarded.

I could hear the road from my foxhole, knew when the dumpers started their trip down the road, bringing more waste and valuta into our republic. I heard the lawnmower engines of the locals' cars and bikes buzz past, the heavy growl of the Robur and the W50 trucks as they drove in and out of the collective farms.

At 0714 a tractor paced the field to the west of the woods, the engine tacking and returning in dull regularity.

By 0932 it had finished and the lorries on the road returned to the main stage.

At 1007 the blast of turbines morphed into the scissoring rotors of a heavy transport helicopter heading south. Positive identification wasn't possible through the tree canopy.

Seventy minutes later it returned, on a course further east.

At 1406 the high whine of a motorbike sank into a two-stroked clatter as it slowed and stopped.

That was my Simson rider, come to pick up or deliver whatever package Oskar would be stopping for. Before I'd even noted the arrival of the moped in my notebook, a diesel engine came up the road. Instead of dopplering past, it stepped down through the gears and died away in a hiss of hydraulics.

A door slammed and dead leaves swished. The truck had stopped much closer to the clearing than the moped and I swung the glasses to the north to await Oskar's arrival. He had a cigarette in his gob as he came down the path, his head swivelled around in short jerks as he checked the empty space in the woodland. Noting the absence of his contact, he turned and headed back up the path he'd just come down.

The brisk shuffle of fast steps on the other path caught my attention, I swung the binoculars around, ready to catch sight of the contact. He was moving fast, running after Oskar, head down, keeping an eye on the uneven forest floor.

From my elevated position I could see only his white motorbike half-helmet and grey-clad torso as he sprinted through the clearing after Oskar. My field glasses remained trained on the path they'd disappeared down, even when I heard Oskar's truck start up and drive off.

Thirty seconds later, the Simson started up, its chattering engine settling to a steady high pitch as it pulled away. The contact must have walked back along the road rather than through the forest.

That was it. Nine hours hocking in this dirt hole and I didn't even get a good look at Oskar's contact.

I collected my motorbike and headed back to my billet. I was tired and my limbs were stiff, but before I could rest, I had another job to do.

I wrote my message in tiny letters, written on a strip cut from the bottom of a fine sheet of typewriter paper. The paper was then wrapped around a hair grip and pushed into the broken pen I used for the dead drop. I was ready for my walk along the tree lined road to Motzen.

The pen went into a crook of the roots of the old oak tree, a quick scuff of my boot and it was under curled brown leaves. I walked away, leaving my message.

Keine besondere Vorkommnisse. Nothing to report.

41
GALLUN

After a bit of a nap I took the Trabi up to Berlin. There were a few things I needed to do, but first I wanted to check what level of security the major thought I was worth.

I came off the autobahn at Waltersdorf and took the bridge over the motorway, heading north-west, into the sticks. It's a dead-straight road, over a kilometre to the village of Kienberg, which sits on a hairpin bend and boasts two dirt roads and a handful of holiday shacks. From the motorway bridge it's a two-minute drive until you reach where the road bends around the back of the village. I parked down a track that runs between the houses, a gap between two bungalows boasted a perfect view of any traffic heading towards the village.

This was one of the best places I'd found to break a box or any other clever mobile surveillance techniques—there's only one route in and I had that covered.

After ten minutes no other traffic had made its way down the cobbled road. Looked like I was clean.

I fired up the Trabant again and pointed it down field tracks and lanes around the back of Schönefeld airport.

Turning onto the main road, I headed into Berlin, still keeping a wary eye on the rear-view mirror. Leaving the car in Friedrichshain, I jumped onto the S-Bahn at Frankfurter Allee. I travelled four stops in one direction, then back one.

By now I was convinced the major wasn't having me followed. At least not today.

★

A block away from Greifswalder Strasse S-Bahn station, you'll find the State Ballet School. From the outside it looks like any other polytechnic secondary school. The mosaic by the entrance is your first clue that this place might be a bit different. Broken tiles set into concrete show a pair of dancers. The strength of youth. The future of Socialism. Some such guff.

Go past the Socialist Realist artwork, walk up the seven steps to the front door and turn right. Ignore the leotarded youth with their buns permanently stapled to the back of their heads, don't let all the preening and oh-gosh-ing get to you, you're nearly there.

Head up the stairs and past three doors. The fourth door is a little smaller, announcing a storage cupboard. Take the key out of your pocket, let yourself in, twist the light switch until the neon tube fizzes into life. Behind the boxes of plimsolls and dancing slippers there are damp patches where the plaster has fallen off the wall. Second shelf down, on the right, a particularly bad area of dermatitis has claimed the pointing of the bricks. Insert a knife, an alloy jobbie from the canteen will do it, lever out a brick. Hand in, pull out steel box.

Another key opens the emergency stash. Polish passport, Yugoslav passport and a stack of blue tiles that had made their way to me after interrogations of Westerners at border crossing points. I flicked through and pulled out ten of the blue hundred Westmark notes and stuck them in my pocket. Reverse the above procedure until you find yourself on the platform at the S-Bahn station wondering how to kill the time you've got until dark.

Like so many of life's questions, the answer lies in the bottom of a glass.

42
KÖNIGS WUSTERHAUSEN

The bottom of the glass is also where I found *Unterleutnant* Strehle of Königs Wusterhausen county criminal police.

When I entered the Seven Steps bar near Königs Wusterhausen train station, he was at his usual table near the back. I picked up a couple of beers from the bar and took them to Strehle.

"You owe me more than a beer," he griped as I set a glass in front of him.

"That's not the way to greet an old friend."

Strehle finished his beer and picked up the fresh glass. He paid his respects to it and by the end of the introductions the glass was half-empty. He wasn't a full glass kind of guy.

"We've only just got rid of your lot," he moaned. "Clogging up the police station, asking questions no police officer should ever have to answer. And here you are again: trouble just came waltzing in, expecting to be greeted with open arms."

"I had it worse," I told him.

"Is that so? But you're here now. I'm not going to ask what you want because you'll tell me anyway. But first, get some of the serious stuff in."

I signalled the barman, finger and thumb held apart, the height of a measure of schnapps. He took the bottle of *Doppelkorn* from the shelf behind the bar and set two glasses ready for pouring.

"Oh, just bring the damn bottle over!" Strehle shouted.

The barman shrugged, picked up the glasses and the bottle

and headed our way.

"I can come again if this is a bad time," I offered.

"It's not the timing that bothers me."

Fair enough.

I poured the drinks and we downed them. No toast.

"That team, the surveillance team you sorted for me in September?" I asked Strehle.

"If you're in trouble again, then you're on your own. Forget about me. Walk out of here so I can go back to pretending I've never heard of you." Strehle took the bottle of schnapps and poured himself another. "That way, everyone stays alive," he added.

"I came prepared," I offered.

"You came prepared in September. But what you had on me last time has been cancelled out by what I've got on you now. They gave me a number, it's right here in my pocket, a direct line to one of your lot." Strehle paused long enough to fire up a cigarette. He didn't offer me one. "One call and your comrades from the Firm will be down here to haul you off. I'll get my peace and quiet, and on top of that I'll have a nice little bee stamp on my report card. What's not to like?"

I took a file out of my bag. Buff-coloured, the name of the manufacturer, Robotron, printed along the bottom, dotted lines above that so the secretary could fill in the file reference number. I put it on the table and slid it over to the policeman.

He looked at it with one eye, not trusting me enough to go ahead and open it. This country runs on files and registries. Everything bad that can happen to you either starts with a file or ends up in a file. Couldn't blame Strehle for being a bit leery.

"Go on, it won't bite."

Strehle turned the file around so it opened towards him and lifted the flap. He glared at the five blue tiles for a moment, as if challenging them to start moving about. "Worth that much to you?"

I nodded.

"If it's only worth five hundred then you won't need my help." His beer glass was empty now, even though he'd been mostly concentrating on the spirits.

I waved at the barman. He started working on the new beers.

"Call it a down payment," I told Strehle.

"What do you need? Same as last time?"

"Pretty much. Three, four days. Couple of hours each day until we hit the jackpot, then whatever it takes."

"That won't go far when it's split up among the lads," he prodded the folder.

"More where that came from."

"Was hoping you'd say that," Strehle responded.

This time I got a toast when the beers arrived.

43
MITTENWALDE

We were in place by 1300 hours the next day. One vehicle was at the dairy farmyard where a thousand years ago I'd spent all afternoon waiting for Codename Oskar to go past. I was with one of Strehle's men in a Wartburg further down the road towards Mittenwalde, outside the allotment gardens. Another couple of men were crouching in the ditch I'd spent yesterday morning in.

We were in radio contact with each other, and from where I was sitting I could see the registration number of each lorry as it headed towards us.

At 1500 hours I sent the men home. It was a no-show, we'd try again the next day.

The preparations finally paid off the following Monday. At 1357 the radio crackled: *Anton, heading east*

That was Oskar in his truck, coming our way. The driver turned the key and the Wartburg's three cylinders fired up, one after the other.

Shortly after, another report came over the air: *Berta, heading east*

"Silver S51," I told the driver. He already knew what we were looking for, but sometimes I get excited.

"Konrad zwo, pick up Ludwig eins and zwo and follow on," I said into the radio microphone.

Understood

Oskar's orange lorry rumbled past, a couple of minutes

later we heard the buzzing of the Simson. We eased out of the allotment colony, turning left and following the moped towards Mittenwalde. Our little convoy turned onto the bypass, Oskar in his orange truck leading the way, the motorbike following a long way behind, our Wartburg a few hundred metres further back. Out of sight but bringing up the rear, the Konrads in their Lada. Oskar reached the junction with the F246, turning left, towards the landfill. Behind him, the Simson turned right, towards Zossen. We followed the motorbike westwards, it kept at a steady forty-five kilometres per hour, a bit slow for us, but there was enough oncoming traffic to hinder overtaking, so staying back wasn't conspicuous.

After the village of Telz the traffic cleared and we were obliged to pull out and overtake the Simson. Konrad zwo had caught up with us by then and they slotted in behind the motorbike.

"Next pass in Zossen," I told the radio as we pulled ahead.

I kept the motorbike in my mirror for as long as I could, but the trees lining the road meant any slight change in direction hid the traffic behind us.

"Put your foot down, we'll wait in a side road somewhere before we get to the junction with the F96," I told the driver.

He didn't have to do anything he wasn't already doing. We were travelling a steady seventy-five kilometres per hour, heading for Zossen. We parked by the church, just before the junction where the F96 heads west to avoid the Soviet base. We kept the engine running, waiting for notice of the motorbike's approach.

Now in Zossen. Passed water tower, chirped the radio.

They were just six or seven hundred metres away, I kept my eyes on the mirror, waiting for them to come around the bend.

Berta turned left, direction south, residential area

"Turn around, turn around!" I commanded. The driver was already pulling out into the road, ignoring the traffic. With another jerk of the wheel, we were heading back the way we'd just come.

Berta left again after hospital, direction south-south-east

We turned right, passing the hospital on the other side. A road joined from the left, down which Berta and Konrad zwo had just come. Sixty metres ahead of us, the road forked again.

"Which way at the fork? Which way?" I demanded of the radio. I had a compass in my hand, but the needle was swaying around as the car jumped over potholes and uneven cobbles.

We came to a halt at the junction, I pulled the map open, trying to work out which lane headed south-south-east.

"Which way?" I asked again.

Restricted area, entering restricted area, the radio told me instead of answering my question.

"*Scheiße!* Abort! Repeat abort and return!" I shouted into the radio.

Understood

The driver looked at me, trying to understand my nervousness. His eyes followed mine to the map on my lap, to where my finger was held at the intersection of this lane and the red line marking the edge of the Soviet Army base.

44
ZOSSEN

I sent the Konrads back to Königs Wusterhausen and walked into the centre of Zossen. I found the dive I'd been to that rainy night a million years ago, before I'd ever heard of Major Blecher or Codename Oskar. I've had difficult cases before. I've had dangerous cases before. The best cases are a mix of both—anything else bores you after a few years in this job.

But if Major Blecher walked into the bar at that moment, I would have given him back his mission.

Some trouble is too much to take.

Some trouble is worse than a lifetime of spying on manual labourers at a toxic waste dump.

45
ZOSSEN

I left the bar before it got too dark and walked back to the junction where we'd stopped. This time I chose the left fork, where Konrad zwo had followed the motorcyclist. Just a hundred metres further on, a sign warned of the restricted area in Russian, English, French and, finally, German. Ignoring the sign, I continued down the track, entering the woodland. There was no fence, only silence surrounded me.

Fallen pine needles drifted into the ruts left behind by tracked vehicles and heavy tires. I walked down the middle strip where the ground hadn't been so badly cut up. Fresh tire tracks could be seen here, a three-point turn that edged off the track and into the soft sand to the side. This is where Konrad zwo had turned around.

Another hundred metres and the path was barred by a red and white painted boom. A half-rotten sentry hut stood to the left, as empty as the woods around me.

At the other side of the road, churned sand showed where the bike had gone around the gate. I knelt down and, with the aid of a torch held low to show up the ridges and indentations, examined the tracks. There were several sets of tyre imprints to be seen, this route was used often, either by the S51 we'd followed or by other motorbikes with similar width tires.

It took me two hours to walk back to my lodging and another half an hour to decide what message to leave for Major Blecher in the dead drop.

In the end I settled on another *Nothing to report*. I had no illusions that my lapidary dispatch would buy me much time, Blecher was hoping for an enhanced report, one with lots of action in it. If I couldn't provide him with some interesting material before his patience ran out then he'd pass me back to Captain Funke and my cadre file would be closed for good.

But today the game had changed, my mission was a lot more serious than I'd realised. It wasn't merely an investigation with the potential to start a turf-war between Stasi departments, this case had a serious Soviet connection. Bad for your life expectancy, that kind of thing.

Unable to work out my next steps, I went to bed. After the day I'd just had, I decided I needed to do something for my health. But I was too tired to sleep. So I lay under the covers and thought.

So far I had one or two waste lorry drivers who smuggled and another lorry driver who was doing something but I didn't know what. I also had two bosses, one of whom was keen for more interesting reports. And don't forget the light motorcycle registered to a Border Regiment but last seen driving into a Soviet restricted area.

The safest thing for me to do would be to find some irregularities at the Intershop, find, build or fake a little bit of evidence against Detlef the smuggler and call it a day.

Do that and Major Blecher would hopefully lose interest while Captain Funke might be pleased enough for me to persuade him to transfer me out of this shithole. My next posting would probably be only slightly better, breathing in traffic fumes on twelve hour shifts at a motorway border checkpoint, something like that. But I'd still be alive.

Or, I could keep schtum about the mysterious motorcycle's destination and try to persuade Major Blecher to focus on Oskar. I'd go on another trip to West Berlin and sit in a bar while I was over there. Enhance some reports, dream up a juicy plot for Oskar. What did I care if they took him out? It would mean a gold star for me, and the hope that the major would keep to his unspoken word and get me transferred to a better posting.

Satisfied with the plan, I went back out into the night and replaced the message in the dead drop.

Oskar active. Verbal report necessary.

46
BERLIN KÖPENICK

"Codename Oskar met with an unknown person? Any exchanges?" The major lifted himself out of the easy chair. He'd come to the safe flat in Köpenick on a weekday morning, but I was making it worth his while.

"Yes, Comrade Major. Oskar handed over a small packet, approximately one hundred and fifty millimetres by two hundred and-"

"What did they say? Any challenge and response? Any conversation?"

"No, Comrade Major. It was my impression that the two subjects knew each other."

"Potential for use of operative-technical resources?"

"Far from ideal, Comrade Major. The subjects were constantly moving. A static listening device would have trouble receiving while difficult terrain restricts the operational efficacy of directional technology."

Blecher resumed his pacing, his brow creased in thought. "You're sure it was the same motorbike?" He stopped by the window and turned to me.

"Comrade Major, from my position I couldn't see the vehicle, I only heard it. Small engine, two-stroke. Could be anything from a Schwalbe to an S70."

The Comrade Major didn't know his motorbikes, I could have compared the little Simson to an Ural and he would have given me the same knowledgeable nod. He resumed his pacing in front of the window.

"Comrade Major, the answer lies in West Berlin. Whatever was in that package, we need to know its origin."

"Yes, yes," said the major. He went to the door, issued instructions to the goon standing outside and went back to the window. "The packet you saw—could it have been a video cassette?"

"More like two, Comrade Major," I answered, diligently enhancing my already enhanced information.

But while I was busy giving my report, my mind was replaying yesterday's scene. The Konrads had been in the clearing, in the same observation position I'd used. Nevertheless, they hadn't actually seen the meeting between Oskar and his contact. Oskar had walked into the clearing and, not seeing his contact, had headed up the path towards where the motorbike was parked. Less than a minute later, he returned through the clearing on the way back to his lorry.

"Very well. Comrade Reim," said Blecher after staring out the window for a minute or two. "You go over tonight."

"I'll need technical equipment," Blecher switched his attention from the window back to me. His brow was creased again. "Carrier bug for Oskar's living room, Comrade Major. And an audio cassette player."

There was silence while he thought this over. Practically speaking, I was asking for first sight of material recorded in Oskar's flat, and that would give me a measure of independence from my handler while I was in the operational area.

The major went to the door again, opened it slightly and issued an order. He shut the door before speaking. "We'll send you over with a microphone and five hundred Westmarks. I want you to keep proper accounts this time."

47
WEST BERLIN
Wedding

I made the crossing the same night, at about the time Oskar would probably be shuffling between his flat and the bar.

The actual passage through the restricted zone and onto the platform at S-Bahn station Wollankstrasse was uneventful. There was no cop standing on the road outside the station this time, although two of them were in a marked car parked near the junction. Watching rush-hour commuters seemed to be standard practice over here.

There was no food in Gertrud's flat, nor was there any Gertrud for that matter, so it was just me and the few bottles of beer still left in the fridge. I made myself comfortable in front of the black and white portable, popped a beer and watched Dallas on a West German channel.

When I woke up in the armchair it was light outside and a church service was on the telly. I switched it off sharpish.

Another beer from the fridge, then I began work at the kitchen table, writing down ideas on paper, then scribbling them out again. I was working on two separate pieces of paper. On one sheet I was working out what I could tell Major Blecher. The other was for me to try to make sense of what was actually happening around Oskar and the S51 moped.

By two o'clock, the grumblings in my belly were getting in the way of my thinking, so I headed out in search of food. I found a *Currywurst* booth, ate two standing at the counter, a bottle of Schultheiss pilsner keeping the sausage company as it went down, then I bought a couple more bottles to take back to the flat.

The next morning I was sitting in the green Opel on Oskar's street, waiting for him to try to remember where he'd left his car. I took him to work, waiting outside as he clocked on and got into his lorry.

He headed towards Zehlendorf, I went back to Kreuzberg.

This was getting to be a routine.

I let myself into Oskar's flat, opened up the receiver on his telephone and slid the new microphone into place, I wound the wires around the telephone connection, then went down to the cellar to change the tapes on the cassette recorder. With the carrier bug I'd just fitted, we'd be able to hear not only phone calls but also anything said in the same room as the phone.

On the way out, I popped into the cellar and changed tapes. I was done here, it was time for some Western consumerism.

I found a Hertie department store on the other side of the Landwehrkanal from Hallesches Tor and my first stop was the electronics department. I wasn't going to be allowed to take any of this equipment home so I chose a basic model tape player, picked up a pair of headphones and added a few blank cassettes.

"That'll be a hundred and twenty-nine Marks and thirty-three Pfennigs," said the nice young lady at the counter.

"Can you give me a written receipt for a bit more?" I asked, getting my wallet out.

"But the till receipt won't match …" She'd fetched the receipt block from beneath the counter and her pen hovered above it uncertainly.

"That's fine, I just need something with a stamp on it." I put a hundred and fifty Marks on the counter.

The cashier looked around nervously. What was her problem? Did no-one in West Berlin fiddle their expenses?

"How about," I leant over the counter and lowered my voice, scooting the notes over as I did so. "How about you 'forget' to write the amount in, just do the stamp? And keep the change."

"Oh, I couldn't possibly do that!" redness was spreading up her neck and over her cheeks.

She put the items in a bag and added the receipt with a wink.

I checked when I got outside, I had a receipt, HERTIE printed at the top, a rubber stamp at the bottom and all the lines in between were empty.

I took my purchases back to the flat in Wedding, and mostly out of curiosity, I slotted home the tape I'd retrieved earlier from Oskar's cellar.

While I packed away the rest of the shopping—coffee, more beer, a bottle of vodka, some basic foodstuffs—I let the tape rewind. With a whine it hit the end and I pressed stop, then play.

Schraber. Oskar's voice.

It's me, just phoning you about next Sunday. A woman's voice, rusty, but not ancient. Relaxed, using the familiar *Du.* His mother.

I put my forefinger on the play button and pressed the FF button with my middle finger, listening to the squeaky sounds for a second or two before taking my fingers away.

I'll call you about next weekend, bye Mutti.

Click-click.

Ringing tone. Pause. Ring.

Hier Schraber, ja bitte?

Thursday. Just overnight this time, said the next caller. Speaking good German, he convincingly negotiated most of the consonants and vowels but got hung up on the Rs, they were far too flat.

Understood, just the one night, replied Oskar and hung up.

I pushed the pause button down, thought about what I'd heard, then replayed the conversation. English maybe? Or American? Definitely not a native German speaker.

But the caller's linguistic origins weren't my main concern. Oskar was doing another delivery to Schöneiche tomorrow, even though it was only a couple of days since his last trip.

That was a break in his pattern.

And what did *overnight / the one night* mean? Did it mean go there Thursday and again on Friday? In that case, why didn't the caller just say *Thursday and Friday* or *Thursday and again the next day* or any one of the hundred different ways of saying it more clearly?

Why *overnight?* There was no overnight, Oskar had to be back over the border and tucked up in bed before the gates at the crossing point shut at 2300 hours.

48
WEST BERLIN
Wedding

"Aunt Hilde? I'm taking the shopping home," I told the telephone receiver. I was in a call box in Tegel, about six kilometres away from the safe flat. A safe distance, I thought.

"It's your sister's turn," replied Hilde. It was a different Hilde again, this one had an aggrieved tone of voice.

"Please let my sister know she should do more shopping. I'll see her at the shops later." I hung up before Hilde could respond. It was already getting dark as I walked to the S-Bahn station. The lights from cars and shops made the modern shopping precinct look homely, something it never did in the harsh light of day. I alighted at Wollankstrasse and let the platform manager know that I was here and intending to go further. He wound a telephone and communicated with someone at Friedrichstrasse station and told me to go and sit in the waiting room. Half an hour later he gave me the signal, it was time to go.

Still wearing the army fatigues after crossing the Wall, I wandered around Pankow until I found a call box. I put a twenty pfennigs coin in the slot and dialled the Seven Steps bar in Königs Wusterhausen.

"Give Strehle a message, tell him it's tomorrow. He'll understand," I said to the barkeeper and hung up.

I'd gone to a lot of trouble to get in touch with the

policeman. While it was technically possible to have called from West Berlin, the message would have been picked up by my colleagues in the Firm. This way may be a hassle but it was safer. On the other hand, I now had to justify to the major why I was back in East Berlin.

Major Blecher was waiting for me in the damp flat. He was pacing up and down as he had done on Tuesday, as if unaware of the passage of time.

"Well, what have you got?"

I felt sorry for him. All I had was a tape and the news that Oskar was about to go on a trip tomorrow. I dressed it up as much as I could. "Oskar has received instructions. This is a complete change from his previous operational pattern."

"Yes, yes ..." said the major, as if it were all his idea.

"He picked up a parcel during the course of his normal work activities this morning. It is a matter of operational significance that we gain and keep awareness of the whereabouts of that parcel."

"I see ..."

"We need round-the-clock surveillance of Oskar from now until at least the end of the week."

"In the operational area?"

"In West Berlin, yes. We can't efficiently cover the surveillance between the two of us."

"Make contact tomorrow morning, I'll see what I can do."

Wool successfully pulled over the major's eyes, I returned to West Berlin. This time there were no cops outside the station. The whole place was quieter, not so many passengers at this time of night.

I walked back to the Kadett parked near the safe flat, taking a few wrong turns, staring into shop windows and tying a few too many shoelaces on the way. No tail.

★

"Anything at all?" I asked Gertrud as I got into her red Volkswagen outside Oskar's flat.

"Came home after work, went shopping at the supermarket around the corner. Hasn't been out since."

"No trips to Malheur?" Gertrud shook her head. She hadn't taken her eyes off the front door of Oskar's tenement block since she'd first clocked me in the mirror.

"Can you stay here tonight?" I asked. Gertrud nodded. "And tomorrow evening?"

"I'll be here from 2300 hours," she responded, eyes still fixed on the front door down the street.

I relieved her at five the next morning. There were no parking spaces available, so I took her spot once she'd driven off.

The boredom of surveillance is something you get used to. Your mind shuts down but the eyes remain alert for movement, any movement.

It's not just the door to Oskar's building you need to remain aware of, it's the dog walkers, the children on the way to school, the cop or the traffic warden. The neighbour hoping to hook the few metres of the street you're parked on, or the postal worker on his overladen bicycle. Any of these may notice you, think it odd and report what they'd seen.

Other than being aware and ready with a plausible excuse, there's not much you can do in close urban environments.

If this operation continued for much longer we should try to gain access to a place opposite Oskar's building, settle ourselves into the attic, lift a tile if there's no handy window. But that requires a bigger team, one to watch and one to remain out of sight and on standby with a vehicle.

My first sighting of Oskar that day was at 0816 when he went for bread rolls. Whether it was because he'd had a lie-in, or whether it was because he hadn't spent last night drinking in the Malheur I don't know, but he was steady on his pins this morning.

I followed him on foot as he walked around the corner to the Turkish bakery on Zossener Strasse. I stood on the other side of the road, outside a comic shop, as he chatted with the woman behind the counter. Finally, she put three rolls and a börek in two paper bags and received a handful of change in return. I housed him and got back behind the wheel of the Opel, wishing I'd had the foresight to bring some bread rolls too. I unscrewed my flask of coffee and made do with that.

The next sighting came at 1112 hours. Oskar got into his car and took the two corners to Gneisenaustrasse. On to Mehringdamm, up to the canal, then through the Tiergarten to the roundabout with the Victory Column in the middle— moved there by Hitler in 1939, since when nobody ever saw fit to pull it down again. From there it was a straight run to the Congress Centre and a right turn to Ruhleben.

I waited outside the gates of the waste incinerator while Oskar went into the offices to do whatever he had to do. He came out with keys in his hand and headed towards the lorry park. He wasn't as steady on his legs as this morning, his steps came jagged. Nervous. As well he should be.

I kept him company as far as I could, taking my leave just short of the border crossing in Lichtenrade. From there he'd have to go the next kilometre by himself, although the border guards would look after him, and after that the Konrads would be keeping an eye out.

I parked up by the side of the road and slipped back into patience mode.

49
WEST BERLIN
Kreuzberg

Oskar returned nearly two hours later. I checked my watch, noted the time in my notebook and turned the ignition.

I wasn't in communication with the Konrads on the other side so didn't know how his trip to Schöneiche had been, not even whether he'd stopped at the small woodland on the way. All I knew was that his truck and trailer had re-entered West Berlin and were heading north.

It was the same procedure as last time, take him up to the incinerator in Ruhleben, wait for him to clock off and get into his own car.

When the burgundy Ford drove past, I pulled into the traffic and followed as he drove onto the Stadtring autobahn. I was relaxed, I knew the route he'd take to get home. All I had to do was house him and make my report.

But Oskar soon woke me up. Instead of continuing around the Stadtring, he came off the motorway at Halensee. By driving through the quiet streets of Grunewald he was making my job as difficult as it could be. Wide roads with plenty of junctions, little traffic underway. I had to hang a block or two back, always running the risk he'd drive around a corner and no longer be there when I got that far. He hesitated at crossroads and corners, took multiple right turns and travelled down the same stretch of road several times.

He was good, I really couldn't tell you whether he was

being very subtle in his dry-cleaning or genuinely had no clue where he was. Just as I was coming down on the side of sophisticated counter-surveillance, the Ford Taunus pulled to the side of the road, outside a particularly frilly *Jugendstil* house. I continued past him and took the next side road, parked up and sprinted back to the corner in time to see his head of grey hair being admitted to the oversized chalet. I ran back to my car, reached in and took out a dog lead, then briskly made my way down the street, looking for naughty Fido who had managed to slip his leash again.

Like all the other dwellings around here, the villa was surrounded by a generous garden. A high iron fence topped with sharp spikes from another age surrounded the grounds and a gate, operated via an intercom system, controlled access to the front door.

Another set of gates, also remotely controlled, allowed access to the ramp to an underground garage beneath the house.

I carried on walking, pondering my lack of options, when I noticed a narrow path between the fences of two houses. Considering it to be the kind of path Fido might have liked to explore, I decided to go for a look.

The track led down to a lake, one of the shallow glacial scars that you get in this part of the world. What I liked about this lake was the way the path continued along the shore and around the back of the houses I'd just passed.

I counted the buildings and examined the fence of the third one along. Same gold-tipped cast iron spears as at the front, but fewer people to take notice of me if I decided to take my chances.

I rooted around in the undergrowth, found a stick and lobbed it over the fence onto the lawn, waiting to see if any of Fido's cousins were in the garden. No sounds of barking or panting, no blood-curdling growls. That was good enough for me.

A few metres further, a bent and broken willow provided a step up to the fence and I made use of it.

It was while I was peering through the gaps in the bars, planning my next move and all the while wishing I'd brought the field glasses, when the dog walker appeared.

"Young man!" she had a shrill voice but her Pekingese's yapping was even shriller. "What do you think you're doing? Come down at once or I'll phone the police!"

She was already backing off, on her way home to give the bulls a ring.

There's not a lot you can do in these situations. The last thing I needed was the West Berlin police taking an interest. I jumped off the low branch, held my empty leash out and tried to explain. "My pooch got through the fence, I think he's in there."

"Well, why didn't you say so? I'm sure that young man in the garden will be able to help." She used her sharp nose to indicate the figure that had materialised on the other side of the fence.

Flannel shirt, sports jacket, tell-tale bulge under left armpit. Since he'd already clocked me, I had nothing to lose, so I tried to chat him up.

"Walking my neighbour's dog." I held up the guilty lead again. "It somehow got free and ran this way, I think it may be in your garden." I peered through the fence, checking the tailored lawns for the missing hound.

The fellow in the sports jacket didn't answer. He just stood there like a stuffed bouncer, hands clasped below his stomach.

"Do you think I could come in, see if I can find the dog?"

He gave me a look that would have frozen a Medusa and did an about-turn before walking back to the house.

As he did his smart twist, the jacket flapped open giving me a view of his hardware. The sharp tang and the length of the grip told me he was wearing a Browning HP, the pistol so beloved by several NATO armed forces.

50
WEST BERLIN
Grunewald

If I'd thought the silent guard in the garden rather rude, the two men behind me were even ruder. Just like their colleague on the other side of the fence, they didn't have anything to say to me. They didn't need to, the bulges under the left armpits did all the talking.

Just like sheepdogs, they herded me back down the path and onto the street. I was walking in front of them, protesting at my treatment and trying to get them to say something. Anything. A single word might be enough to nail down their nationality. But they remained silent and I allowed myself to be escorted to the bus stop on Hubertusallee, where they stood around like sphinxes until I got on the next bus.

The bus drove off, with me on the back seat, looking at the scene I was leaving behind. The two goons were returning the way they'd come.

That was some heavy security and their reluctance to speak coupled with the choice of goon No. 1's weapon suggested I hadn't met the West Berlin police, who were issued with the Sig P6.

I got off at the next stop and, doing my best to remain out of sight, found my way back to the car. I had no idea whether Oskar or anyone else had left the house while I was indisposed, but me and the Kadett moved ourselves further along the road anyway. Far enough to not stand out, but still in the line of sight of the front gates of the house.

I had a long wait, it wasn't until 1953 hours that there was any movement from the *Jugendstil* villa. A West Berlin registered silver VW Scirocco passed me and waited for a moment outside the house before it was admitted to the driveway. Ten minutes later, the car emerged and turned my way.

As it passed, I peered over the dashboard, hoping to see the passengers. The driver was a further variation on the goons I'd just met. In the dim light of the streetlamps I hadn't been able to see the occupants of the rear seat.

As the car pulled onto Hubertusallee and headed north, towards the motorway, I got my Opel warmed up and headed after them. A few moments of ignoring traffic regulations and I had them back in sight.

It was tricky. The traffic grew heavy once we'd left the posh villas behind and I was worried about losing them. But they'd pick me out soon enough if I got too close. I'd already experienced their security and I doubted they'd be so friendly the next time we met.

I managed to keep tabs on the Scirocco as it crossed over Heerstrasse, heading towards Ruhleben. But much sooner than I expected, the car turned left—heading directly towards the Olympia complex. I took them as far as Olympischer Platz where they headed right and I took a discreet left. This was as far as I could go, any further and I would have run over the sentry at the gate of the British occupation forces HQ.

I was doing well finding my way back to the main road but was uncomfortable about the number of uniformed British Army soldiers around the place. This was their part of Berlin, I was driving through the quarters for officers and their families, oncoming traffic was mostly made up troop carriers, Land Rovers and other military vehicles. This was the last place I needed to be.

The traffic lights at the junction to Heerstrasse were up ahead, another few metres and I'd be back in the relative normality of civilian West Berlin.

As the lights turned amber I eased up on the accelerator. A heavy Mercedes nipped in front of me and, already nervous, I quickly scanned my mirrors. Another Mercedes behind me, one more coming up on my outside. The car in front halted sharply so I hit the brakes. Before I'd even come to a complete stop, the car door was ripped open.

Two Browning HP pistols pointed at me, one from the front, through the windscreen, the other through the open door at my side. I kept my hands on the wheel and my eyes on the pistol to my left.

My new friends were cut from the same cloth as those in Grunewald this afternoon. Not a word was spoken, a wave of a pistol was all the invitation I was going to get. I climbed out of the Opel, taking it slow, letting them see both hands at all times. A barrel poked my left kidney while hands searched me. All they found were the keys to the safe flat and a wallet with a few Deutsche Marks and my false West Berlin ID.

Another nudge from a pistol steered me towards one of the Mercedes and an open door to let me know I was expected. As I was shoved into the back-seat, I saw one of the goons get into my green Kadett. I saw the traffic lights change but I saw no more. A sack had been pulled over my head as our little convoy moved off.

51
UNKNOWN

The journey in the car took about half an hour and was followed by two steps up and twenty-seven steps down, a rough hand on my shoulder to guide me.

When they took the sack off, I still couldn't see much of my current surroundings. A bright spotlight was pointed directly at me and the walls to either side were in shadow. When I tried to turn my head to try to see more, a pair of hands locked around my head, fingers digging into the soft areas behind my jaw.

I closed my eyes, they let me do that, but bright orange bled through my eyelids and made me want to look again. And when I did, that bright bulb was waiting, ready to burn through my retinas.

They kept me like that for a while. Less than an hour? More than three hours? I don't know.

The hands grasped my head whenever I tried to turn away from the light, the fingers digging into my face a bit harder each time. No word was spoken, no questions asked.

At some point a door opened behind me, heavy, hinges that sounded like a cat on heat. Shuffling steps, again the squeal of the door, the clunk as it settled into its frame. I turned my head to look and this time, no hands clutched my jaw to point me back to the light. But I was still tied to a chair that was in turn fixed to the floor and I couldn't twist my neck far enough to see if anyone was there.

The walls were roughcast, most of the whitewash was worn

away, showing grey mottled with damp. I twisted my neck a little further, a black twisted electrical cable was fixed to the wall, ending in a black Bakelite light switch, the old-fashioned kind that you twist to turn the light on or off. The kind you find in cellars all over central Europe.

There was nothing to tell me where I was. A basement, probably in Berlin. But East or West?

I turned my head the other way, give my other eye a break from the glare. But whatever I did, whichever way I turned, the light was there, out-staring me, stunning my thoughts and feeding on my energy.

The shriek of the door opening had me looking to the front again, marvelling at how well trained I had become in such a short time. Footsteps, more than one pair, yet only one figure moved past me. A grey sweatshirt, dark hair. Short. That was all I saw of him before he moved out of sight behind the lamp. I was ready for the questioning, I'd had time to prepare.

"What were you doing when we picked you up?" It was a steady voice. Strong, but not loud. A clean German accent, no regional tang, which made me think the speaker was probably from West Germany. But I couldn't be sure, it was like any dialect had been deliberately wiped away. A good interrogator's voice.

I didn't answer, just closed my eyes and waited for the blow. It didn't come, no open hand slapped me, no fist knocked me. I opened my eyes again, still nothing to see but the glare from the lamp. When I closed my eyes, nothing to see but the orange corona burnt onto the back of my eyeballs.

OK, not so physical, at least not yet. But another question would come, or the same one again. I sat there, looking down, keeping my eyes closed for as long as I could. Waiting. I tried to distract myself with other thoughts. Like what time was it? It must be gone midnight and I hadn't made contact with Aunt Hilde. They'd be on alert by now. If I didn't check in soon they'd assume I'd gone AWOL again. If I ever got out of here I'd probably have more fun and games waiting for me, courtesy of the Firm.

But I was still waiting for the questions, wondering how long I'd manage to stay quiet. Sure, we'd had training. Resistance to interrogation, they'd called it. And I'd had some recent practice in Hohenschönhausen. Still no fun, though.

The scraping of a chair, the grey figure moved into my range of vision and passed me. The heavy door behind me opened and shut and I was left alone with the bright light.

Glad I wasn't paying their electricity bill.

52
UNKNOWN

They played the game another three or four times. It was getting so old that I was beginning to doze off despite the bright light stuck in my face.

I couldn't feel my hands any more and my legs were cramping up. I tried to straighten them out, but they'd been tied to the chair legs. When did they do that?

Door. Silence. Questioning. Silence. Door.

The door rasped open again, but this time there were no questions. The footsteps told me it wasn't my usual interrogator. Instead of briskly heading for the safety of the shadows behind the lamp, this person came between the lamp and me. I was in the shade and beyond the fact that he was tall and thin, I couldn't make out much about him. But whoever this guy was, my eyes were grateful for the rest.

"Here you are, pal," he said in English, holding a packet of cigarettes my way.

I didn't understand the words, but I wasn't so far gone I couldn't recognise a cigarette when I saw one. I nodded and my new friend fed the nail between my lips and lit me up.

The smoke got in my eyes and I shook my head, trying to clear them. The cigarette fell from my lips, landing on my jumper.

Tall guy saw what was happening and stepped forward, picking up my cigarette and patting at the burn mark.

"Here you are," he repeated as he fed the still-lit cigarette back into my mouth.

I lowered my head and waggled my right hand, as if straining to reach up. He looked at the door, back at my hand and shrugged. What harm could releasing one hand do when the other wrist and both ankles were still attached to the chair? He knelt down beside me and undid the knot.

As soon as my wrist was free, I balled my fist and hit him on the jaw. He still had a cigarette in his mouth and my punch broke his jaw. Sorry, pal, nothing personal, that's just the way it goes.

He fell backwards, losing the cigarette in the process. On the way down, his head hit the edge of the table and he slid the rest of the way to the floor.

Squinting in the light, I rapidly undid my other wrist, then my legs, and stepped forward to pat tall guy down for weapons. He had no gun, they weren't complete amateurs, but I did find a short wooden truncheon in his pocket. Only half marks, then.

I propped the unconscious guard in my chair and pulled the sack over his head, then went to wait behind the door.

It took the other guards about ten minutes to return, I didn't hear them coming, but I saw the handle turn and the door began to open, slowly at first, then faster as momentum gathered. As soon as the first guy was in the room, I coshed him on the back of the neck and threw my weight against the door, shoving it against the second man, catching him on the side of the head. He was dazed, stretching his arms out to steady himself against the wall. I grabbed a wrist, levering his arm around the edge of the heavy door until I heard a crack. The scream came half a second later.

The man with the broken arm slipped to the floor and was giving me the evil eye and whimpering. I stepped over him and through the doorway.

53
UNKNOWN

The corridor was empty, a few doors were shut, steps upwards were at the end. I found the light switch and twisted it to off, then eased my way through the dark and up the steps. At the top, I cracked the door open and peered out. It was still dark, but enough light from windows around me told me I was in the back yard of a tenement block.

There was no movement, just shadows of wheelie bins and broken bikes. Edging my way around the yard I made the main entrance to the building and got out of there.

Walking at a fast pace, not wanting to attract attention by running, I headed down the road, then turned onto a wider avenue. There was nobody around, no cars on the move. The street lamps, the cars and their registration plates told me I was still in West Berlin, but that wasn't my main concern right now.

I slid along the margins of the pavement, steadily putting distance between myself and the cellar.

A car engine cracked the night's silence. I ducked into a doorway as it came closer and shifted down through the gears, the engine growling as it turned a corner, gears stepping back up, heading my way. I peered around the edge of the entry, trying to catch sight of the car as it threaded between the parked vehicles. There it was: a dark Mercedes saloon, similar to the ones that had picked me up near Olympia. I was still watching the approach of the Mercedes when I felt the frigid muzzle of a gun on the back of my neck.

Putting my hands where they could be seen, I turned around. Slowly. It was my night for meeting goons and here was another brace. A different set from the ones I'd left on the floor of the cellar, obviously, but they certainly looked like the same make and model.

They cuffed my hands behind my back and I was encouraged to get in the back of the dark Mercedes that had pulled up and was patiently waiting for us. We didn't travel far, but since I'd no idea where we'd started from that didn't tell me much.

Other than hard smiles and gestures with the barrels of pistols, there was no communication from my captors, but that changed when we pulled through an open gate set into a high brick wall. Small vans were parked around the edge of a concreted yard, a low red-brick office with barred windows huddled at the side.

The Mercedes stopped by the entrance to the building and another goon materialised out of the dimness. "*Vylaz'! Davai.*"

OK, Russian. It was also my night for foreign languages.

My shoulder was grasped and twisted so that my hands were available and I was yanked out of the car by the wrists. My shoulder joints screamed, but my mouth stayed shut.

"*Poshel, tuda!*" A hand on the cuffs steered my trajectory, a yank one way or the other, turning me so I was going in the right direction. A sharp word whenever my guards felt I needed it, a prod in the back to keep me on my toes.

Down a long corridor, wooden doors to either side, worn lino at our feet. A room on the right. Table, two chairs.

Familiar interrogation landscape.

The chair at the window was occupied by a man wearing a shiny face, cropped salt and pepper hair and a well-pressed Soviet Army uniform. He was average height, but wide with it. He had more wrinkles around one eye than the other. The four stars and double gold braid on crimson shoulder boards told me he was a captain of the land forces.

"*Vot plennik, tovarishtch kapitan Pozdniakov!*" shouted the guy who had his hands on my cuffs.

"*Snimite naruchniki i vyidite,*" replied the captain.

I understood well enough what they were saying, but other than turning round to allow the cuffs to be removed, there hadn't been any call for me to respond. Until now.

"Please, sit down," said the captain. It was a polite request, it was in German and I saw no reason not to comply. No lamps pointed my way, no ropes waiting. The goons had been sent away and the good captain already had a deck of cigarettes pointed in my direction. Making myself comfortable on the chair, I took a butt and accepted a light. We smoked, staring across the table at each other. I finished my gasper and reached for another. The captain offered me a light again then stubbed his own cigarette out.

"Comrade Second Lieutenant Reim," he said after I'd got most of my second nail out of the way. If he'd wanted to impress me with that cheap trick, he'd failed.

"Comrade Captain Pozdniakov," I replied. "Assuming the guards addressed you by your real name?"

The captain inclined his head in acknowledgement and we looked at each other for a few more minutes. "Comrade Second Lieutenant, I have a few questions about what's going on in Schöneiche."

"I'm afraid I won't be able to answer any questions unless instructed to do so by my superior officer."

"I don't think we need worry ourselves about the Comrade Major Blecher."

He had my attention now. He knew my name, big deal, just meant he'd seen my mugshot, or there was some list somewhere with my name next to the legend on my fake ID card. But name dropping Blecher was a bit more impressive.

I took another cigarette but didn't spark up for the moment, just rolled it between my fingers. Not many people knew about my connection to the major from Main

Department VIII.

"You're interested in the subject you call Oskar," said the captain.

"If you've got something to say, then just say it," I told him. I'd been playing games with too many people for too long, first the British, now the Russians. "I've run out of patience for tonight."

"We'll talk *Klartext* soon," he was showing off his German idioms now. "But first I have a simple question-"

"I won't be able to answer any questions-"

"Yes, yes. You already said." Captain Pozdniakov waved his fat fingers and looked away in boredom. "Listen to the question before you start defending your chastity. When did you last see Oskar?"

I tapped the unlit cigarette on the table, twisting it round in my fingers, then tapping the other end. The question was unexpected, but I had one of my own:

"Why am I here?"

"All in good time." The wave of the hand again, a disappointed look. "You're here because of me, but we'll come to that. Now, tell me about Oskar."

"Saw him a few hours ago. Entering a villa in Grunewald." That earned me a pleased look.

The captain was watching me again, but his body was angled away, so he had to turn his head my way. It made his eyes seem a little cross-eyed.

"This is how it's going to work, Reim," Pozdniakov fixed his gaze on me. "You go back home and find something else to do. Anything you like, so long as it's got nothing to do with Oskar."

"What do you want me to tell Blecher?"

"Whatever you want. But if you or anyone else continues to take an interest in Oskar then we shall have to meet again. And next time our chat may not be so cosy."

54
BERLIN PANKOW

"Pornographic magazines?" Major Blecher's scepticism could be felt across the room.

"Yes, Comrade Major." I managed to keep a straight face.

"They sent a captain of the Soviet Army to West Berlin to tell you to stop investigating the smuggling of pornographic magazines?"

"Yes, Comrade Major."

Blecher was still concentrating on the obvious, but like a squirrel inspecting empty nutshells on the lawn, sooner or later he'd look up and see the bounty above. I reckoned it would take another minute or two.

"Why didn't they just liaise with whoever it is on our side who deals with this sort of thing?"

"He didn't say, Comrade Major," I said as woodenly as I knew how, all the time watching his face. Here it was, realisation dawning:

"How did they find out about you?" he asked, looking over my shoulder and out of the window. "Did you say this captain knew about me, too?"

"Yes, Comrade Major." He'd finally got there. An unofficial operation, no files, no reports. Limited number of people who even knew that Blecher and I were in any way connected, none of whom knew my rank or name. Yet this Soviet captain pulls me off the street in West Berlin and asks me to pass on his regards to the major.

"Who have you told about this operation?" he demanded,

making an early start at establishing the direction any blame should take.

"Nobody, Comrade Major. Captain Funke isn't aware of your interest. Other than that, I've only had contact with your operative in West Berlin and whoever you've brought to the debriefings, Comrade Major."

"Tell me exactly what this Russian captain said." He pressed his lips together and narrowed his eyes.

"That we have jeopardised an ongoing internal operation and we should cease all operational measures related to Oskar. If we continue, there will be consequences for the Comrade Major."

"And your assessment?"

"The Comrade Captain was wearing the uniform of the Soviet Army," I replied simply. That should be enough for a lowly second lieutenant.

Blecher rubbed his left eye, then snapped out an order: "Return to the landfill at Schöneiche, at least for the time being."

"Permission to ask a question, Comrade Major? What's the operational aim of returning to Schöneiche?"

"Carry on with Operation Magpie, do whatever it is Captain Funke wanted you to do in the first place." Blecher was looking out of the window again. He couldn't wait for me to be gone.

"Comrade Major, smuggling is the only activity of any operational interest-"

"That's for Captain Funke to decide."

Was that it? Blecher was prepared to capitulate to this fastidious Russian captain's demands? And I was to be sent back to snitch on manual labourers on a rubbish tip?

"A suggestion, Comrade Major?" I waited for his nod. "We should continue the observation of Oskar and the evaluation of operational material from Oskar's flat."

The major turned his attention back to me, his head tilted

slightly, like a dog wondering whether it might still be taken for a walk.

"We don't know how Comrade Captain Pozdniakov gained awareness of our operation, but finding out may be necessary for our continued good health."

The major got out of his chair and went to stand by the window, his back to me. After a minute or two, he made a decision.

"OK, find out who the hell Pozdniakov is and why he's interested in us. Do that and I'll get you a permanent transfer away from Main Department VI."

55
District Frankfurt (Oder)

An empty stretch of autobahn to open up the throttle of the MZ, that's the way to clear the mind. I was spending too much time on the details of this case and I still had no sense of the bigger picture. That had to change unless I was prepared to spend the rest of my life as a snitch at Schöneiche.

I headed along the Frankfurt motorway, weaving in and out the convoys of Fiat Polskis heading home. Coming round the tight, cobbled slip road at Fürstenwalde, I took the bike through the wooded Rauen Hills before dropping onto the windy trunk road towards Königs Wusterhausen.

Far as I could work out, there were two routes towards my permanent transfer out of HA VI, and both went through the Russian captain.

If I persuaded Blecher to make the whole Oskar case official —put it on file, develop a formal operational plan, inform the relevant departments—we might succeed in forcing Pozdniakov out of the shadows. He'd have to deal with us on an official level rather than just dragging me off the street at gunpoint.

On the other hand, it may be marginally safer to continue the unofficial investigation. Use my personal connections, see what I could find out about Pozdniakov. Take the new information to Major Blecher and let him take any dangerous decisions.

A convoy of NVA trucks was blocking the trunk road heading west and there were too many to overtake. I'd have to find another route through the sodden countryside. Or I could pull off and have a beer at a local bar.

I got back on the autobahn at Königs Wusterhausen and followed the Berliner Ring round to Potsdam. The two lanes filled and slowed as transit traffic from West Berlin joined us from the border crossing at Drewitz, but it didn't bother me too much, I was coming off at the next junction.

I had just the one task in Potsdam, and it involved a visit to the local headquarters of my own department. Despite pressure from the Ministry's District Administration, Department VI in Potsdam have somehow managed to keep hold of the dilapidated but spacious villa a stone's throw from the Bridge Of Unity, which the *Westler* call Glienicker Bridge.

I showed my clapper board to the sentry at the entrance, then went to see the clerical officer.

"Is *Stabsfeldwebel* Gersch on duty?" I asked.

The clerical officer checked his list and told me Gersch was on the bridge.

A few minutes later, Gersch was welcoming me into his little sentry box, coffee from the flask and brandy from the bottle.

"Cushy number," I observed.

"They let the more experienced troops do the bridge—not much happens here."

I looked out of the window. Access to the bridge was barred by a system of oversized concrete flower pots and fences. Gersch had control of a pedestrian gate that allowed diplomats to pass through to a second hut where papers were checked again. On the other side of the carriageway, the Soviets were responsible for controlling Allied military personnel who wanted to pass over the bridge on their way to or from the various military missions here in Potsdam.

"Chat with them much?" I asked, gesturing towards the Soviet hut.

"Who, the Friends? They'd rather talk to the French than to us Germans."

"You get to see much from here?"

"Nothing else to do. Thinking about anyone in particular?"

"Russians. Get many coming through?" I tried my coffee and added more brandy. A little spirit burner on the floor kept the hut warm.

"The Soviet Consulate-General comes through. Big car, flags on the wings. You interested in him?"

"Any Soviet officers?"

"Had a captain, day before yesterday. Will that do you?"

"Description?"

"So high. Red face, short hair. Everyday uniform, no medals or ribbons. Scarring around his right eye. Came in a UAZ."

"You saw all of that from here?" I asked, peering out of the window again, it was only twenty metres or so to where a jeep would stop at the first barrier, but even if he were in the front seat, the officer would be sitting on the other side of the driver, out of Gersch's line of sight.

"Not the first time he's been through here. Besides, they stopped just over there and waited for the barrier to open. Your captain got out, had a good look around, acted like he owned the place. Then he walked as far as the checkpoint and got in the back of the UAZ. I suppose you'll want to know what he was called?"

"How would you know a thing like that? I thought you just said the Russians won't talk to you?"

"Your man came at just the wrong moment—there was a British mission vehicle coming the other way and they had to manoeuvre around each other." Gersch smiled as he poured more coffee for us both. Making me wait. The highlight of his shift, this would be. "The *Engländer* stopped over there, waiting for the gate to open again. I was standing in the middle, just there, where they'll put the Christmas tree come December. I watched all of this happen, watched the

Engländer come through. The officer in the back was filming me, the NCO in the passenger seat had a microphone in his hand, he was talking into it. 'That's Major Pozdniakov', he said."

"You understand English?"

"No. But I recognise the word *Mädschor* when I hear it. And Pozdniakov isn't exactly English, is it?"

"Sure they said major? Not captain?"

"They definitely called that captain a major. Read it in my report if you like."

56
BERLIN LICHTENBERG

There was no need to check Gersch's report. It's one thing having a chat with an old colleague and asking him to keep it under his hat, another to go marching into the District Administration and leave a record of which files you're interested in. Gersch was getting on a bit, he wasn't far off retirement, but they'd put him in the right place. He might be too old to run after a young man trying to flee the republic, but he was damned good at taking note of what's happening around him.

And thanks to him I now had confirmation of this Russian captain's name: Pozdniakov. Either it was his real name or an alias he used regularly enough to be known by.

A little more detective work and I'd be able to tell you whether he was actually a captain or a major.

Armed with Gersch's confirmation of Pozdniakov's name, I returned to Berlin Centre.

While I was there, I looked up my old friend Holger. I found him hiding in his office.

"What do you want?" he demanded as I appeared in the doorway. I've experienced more enthusiastic receptions.

"You got a moment?"

"You're damaged goods."

"Afraid it'll catch?" Holger and I went way back, I was sure he'd give me a moment of his time. Perhaps.

"Catching? Too late for that. The aggro I got last time I

helped you!" He beckoned me into his office, leant over his desk and whispered. "Half an hour, graveyard opposite."

I gave him a wink and withdrew. I couldn't blame Holger for his caution, word had obviously got around: I was damaged goods.

It was a dull day—one of those days when you're sure the heavy, low cloud that blankets Berlin will never shift. In practice the sun does eventually break through, but not until spring.

I kicked my heels in the park, smoking my cigarettes and watching the grey sky through the bare branches of the trees. I hoped Holger would have the information I needed because I didn't have many other options.

He and I first met at the Ministry school in Golm, both of us still finding our feet in the brave new world of the Ministry. We each recognised the other as a lost soul, and knowing that Vitamin C—personal Connections with a capital C—was what we needed to survive in our new lives, we'd stayed in touch. Along the way we'd given each other a hand, but as Holger had reminded me last time he did me a good turn: the score was heavily weighted towards his side.

"The risk I'm taking just being here!" Holger hissed from behind me.

I turned around and greeted him with a handshake, which he returned without thinking.

"Give me a cigarette," he demanded. He lit up and looked around the graveyard. There was nobody else here, just us, the broken headstones and the weedy trees. This was the kind of place nobody would want to come to.

"Last time you just needed me to do a bit of research in the archives. Nothing sensitive, you said. Well, it was sensitive enough that I had your superior breaking my door down that evening, wanting to know what you were up to. And now there are rumours he's gone missing. What's the news? Has

161

he gone West?"

"Who knows? I'm the last person they'd tell." I shrugged, watching the tip of my own cigarette. I considered Holger a friend, as close a friend as one could have in the Firm. But I wasn't going to tell him everything I knew. That would just scare him off.

"Listen, Holger. You used to be in HA VIII. Know a Major Blecher?"

"Blecher?" Holger tapped the ash off his cigarette and gave the graveyard another once-over. "Which section?"

Good question. I didn't even know which section my handling officer was assigned to.

"OK, where's he based?" asked Holger, still trying to be helpful.

"Not sure. Maybe Köpenick way."

"Technical services, vehicle park, but no administration offices down there. That sound like your man?"

I shook my head. Whatever he did, Blecher did more than command the maintenance of cars and trucks. "OK, here's another name for you: Pozdniakov of the Soviet Armed Forces? Last seen in a captain's uniform of the land forces. Possibly has the rank of major."

"Pozdniakov?" Holger laughed. "You might as well ask me about Major Müller or Sergeant Schmidt!" Slight exaggeration perhaps, but he was right. Pozdniakov is a fairly common Russian surname. But it was worth a try. "As it happens, your Pozdniakov has crossed my radar—if we're talking about the same one. The Ghost Hunter he's called."

"Ghost? As in first-year conscripts in the Soviet Army?" I was thinking of the young lad in the woods that night the Soviet soldiers were searching for porn mags. He'd seemed more frightened than I was, even though he was the one with the gun.

"Maybe. But he's more likely after ghosts of a more substantial kind. He's KGB, but is known to wear an army

162

captain's uniform. That your man?"

"Could be, tell me more." I was getting hopeful again. Always dangerous, a bit of hope.

"Never actually dealt with him, just seen his name in a few reports. Section 5 ran into him a few times, he liked to debrief them after any scrapes they got into while tailing the Allied military liaison missions. Other than that, I guess most contact on our side would be through HV A."

HV A, our foreign intelligence department. They modelled themselves on the Soviet First Chief Directorate and were proud of their independence. Needless to say, I had no Vitamin C there. But Holger's Pozdniakov sounded like a possible.

"I'd like to talk to someone who's actually met him," I told Holger.

"Reim, you can forget about that—I'm done with helping you out. This was just for old time's sake, and now I'm going to take a leaf out of your book and think of number one for a change." Holger dropped his cigarette and stamped on it.

Once again, he was right. I had nothing to offer, I'd already called in all my debts and was running on fumes.

"Right now, I can't offer you anything in return. Maybe something in future," I told him.

I watched him for a moment or two, he was still looking shifty, glancing over his shoulder, checking nobody could see the pair of us together.

"Holger, I'll be straight with you: if I'm wrong about this, I won't be in a position to bother you again. If I'm right then I'll be welcomed back into the fold and you'll be coming to me for favours."

Holger thought about this for a moment.

"I'm not sure which of those options I prefer," he said finally.

57
BERLIN FRIEDRICHSHAIN

We met again the next day. Holger had refused to put me in touch with any of the colleagues from section 5, but he did bring a physical description of Pozdniakov.

"A glass eye?" I asked after listening to Holger's report. "You sure about that?" The other particulars matched, but the glass eye bothered me. If the Pozdniakov I'd met had a false eye I would have noticed.

"It's very realistic. Apparently, this Pozdniakov has a way of staring at you, not moving his good eye so you don't notice the other one doesn't move."

"Tell me more about him."

"Full name Dmitri Alexandrovich Pozdniakov. Don't know date or place of birth. Does liaison mainly, but the stories say he gets involved in active operational measures from time to time. First time his name came across my desk was about four years ago, but it's not the reports that are the most interesting thing about this Russian."

We were sitting in a milk bar on Frankfurter Allee. It was still early afternoon and the place was empty. Having said that, you can never be sure who's listening. But who'd bug a milk bar?

"You mentioned stories?" I said, wondering how how I could get closer to Pozdniakov.

"The glass eye, most of the stories are about the eye," Holger replied.

I still didn't like the glass eye. The Russian, when we met, was in the shadows. I'd noticed a slight squint, dark crows feet which, in hindsight, could have been scars. There'd been a slight inflammation around the conjunctiva that hadn't been matched by reddened sclera, at least, not enough for me to notice in that dark room.

Easy to think of these things afterwards, not so easy to know whether your mind is filling in details after the fact.

"A Soviet conscript went AWOL, tried to get over the border to West Berlin. Pozdniakov brought him in, but not before the soldier had taken Pozdniakov's eye out."

"Should have been more careful. What happened to the soldier?"

"Siberia. But now the conscript also only has one eye. They say after the soldier stabbed Pozdniakov in the face, he took his revenge by scooping out the soldier's own eye and casting it in acrylic."

"He cast a conscript's eye in acrylic?"

"Yup. Uses it as a glass eye."

I sipped my coffee, wondering whether Holger was pulling my leg. I didn't think much of his story—didn't sound plausible for starters. But before I wrote it off I should maybe ask a doctor whether it was even possible.

Or a taxidermist.

58
BERLIN FRIEDRICHSHAIN

What kind of person felt the need to create legends around themselves? Who felt the need to ornament themselves with a violent reputation?

Holger's information was useful, but I still needed to gather more background if I was to work out how the small pieces of intelligence I was gathering could fit together.

The first step was to contact Major Blecher again. I didn't have a direct number for him, I had to go through cut-outs. He liked to pretend he was engaged in conspirational field-work and not just sitting behind a desk in one of the many Ministry offices.

I dialled an internal Ministry number and left a message with a secretary. Ten minutes later, I phoned again to pick up the answer. Obviously it wasn't anything as helpful as Pankow or Köpenick. No, I had to make do with *KW 1* or *KW 2*. This time it was *Konspirative Wohnung 2*, which was the safe flat we'd first used, the one in the newly built Allende Quarter in Köpenick.

When the time came I took my Trabant for the sake of variety. I parked across from the entrance to the block, but instead of going up to the flat, I waited in my car.

Blecher arrived on foot ten minutes later. He was wearing a dark blue suit and a grey anorak and came alone, without the pair of goons who usually followed him around, maybe because it was a weekend.

He went up the steps and let himself into the lobby, then

disappeared from sight. I remained where I was, eyes flicking left to right, then into all three mirrors. Any vehicles entering the courtyard? Any other pedestrians on the move? I stayed in the car for a further five minutes then, having seen nothing interesting, went up to meet the major.

"You're late!" he said as soon as I walked through the door. "You requested this meeting, yet you arrive late."

I didn't bother excusing myself, just told him that I wanted to continue observation of Oskar with the aim of discovering what links, if any, he might have with Pozdniakov.

It took him a while to chew it over, but even then he wasn't swallowing it. "You already have a contact in the operational area. Use her." He meant Gertrud.

"That operative goes to Oskar's tenement every day to change the tapes," I explained. "There's a real risk she's blown by now. I'm definitely burnt. We need further operational personnel if we're to keep tabs on Oskar next time he gets the call."

Blecher knew I was right, but that didn't mean he liked it. Bringing other people in, particularly ones he hadn't personally selected, wasn't part of his plan. He wanted everything kept deniable. If things went wrong it would all be my fault: a known rogue officer in play over in West Berlin. Regrettable, but deniable. But involve too many operatives and it would become that much harder to keep a lid on the whole affair.

"You want to involve another operative?"

"A policeman from one of the districts, I've used him a few times. Very experienced in mobile observation."

Blecher stroked his nose for a while. When he got bored of that he looked out of the window. "And his motivation?"

I rubbed my thumb over my fingertips. The movement made a rasping sound that was nearly as loud as the major's sigh.

"OK, but just this one mission, and you handle him by

167

yourself." Blecher waited until I nodded, then talked about logistics, his favourite topic. "How much does he want?" he asked.

"Five blue tiles should do the job," I answered.

Three hundred Westmarks for Lieutenant Strehle and two for me.

I left the meeting first and waited for Blecher in the Trabant. He took his time coming, perhaps he'd put his feet up, was having another cup of coffee before going back to wherever he came from.

When the major finally appeared, I roused the little two-stroke engine, ready to pull out of the parking space, but the officer sat for a while in his Wartburg, staring out of the windscreen. With a shake of his head, he reached for the ignition, a puff of grey exhaust told me he was about to make a move.

I tailed the Wartburg across the Allende Bridge, nice and smooth, no problems. Once over the river, he turned off to the left, towards the Wuhlheide, where the Ministry's signals intelligence centre is based. But he failed to take the turn-off for the centre, continuing northwards.

Blecher remained a hundred metres in front of me, driving carefully and at a steady pace. The way a man who has nothing to hide would drive.

We ended up in Biesdorf, on the other side of the tracks to Karlshorst and close enough to the zoo to hear the monkeys scream.

It's a strange part of Berlin, like an allotment colony that's mutated, small houses springing up with no concession to planning and order, two-storey semi-detached houses peering over the shoulders of tiny huts built along the edge of the unmetalled lane.

Blecher pulled into the side of the road and got out to open a gate leading to a hammer-plot, a thin drive leading past a street-fronting house, behind which another house sat on its own wedge of land.

The gate open, Blecher drove his Wartburg through and parked by the side of a tidy looking cottage. I went up to the next junction and turned around, parking on the verge for a few minutes before starting the engine again and slowly driving back down the road.

As I passed Blecher's drive, I took a good look at what was going on. The scene was as idyllic as this little garden-town: a little girl, hair done up in braids, was on a red MIFA bicycle, Blecher running along behind, steadying her with a hand on the saddle. The girl was squealing in delight, her mouth wide open revealing the gaps in her row of shining milk teeth. A woman was at the window of the cottage, hair tied back in a ponytail, double chin wobbling as she smiled at the sight of her husband and daughter.

I wanted to make a smart comment about the cosiness of Blecher's Sunday afternoon, even if there was no-one to hear it. But nothing came to mind.

Blecher had everything I'd never had. And it made me dislike him all the more.

59
KÖNIGS WUSTERHAUSEN

I caught up with Strehle in his local, hard by Königs Wusterhausen station. He was in his usual seat, I slid into the chair opposite.

"Don't you have a home to go to?" I asked as I signalled to the barman, another two glasses of beer.

"Have they given you more money to burn?"

"You interested?"

The barman skimmed excess foam from the beers and the policeman drained his glass. He didn't look like he'd been here long, his eyes were still clear, the pupils reacting quickly as his gaze shifted.

The beers arrived and we clinked glasses. He downed half a glass without coming up for air, I took mine more slowly. I'd have to practice if I wanted to keep up with Strehle's intake.

"I don't know if I am interested," he said after wiping the foam moustache off his upper lip. "Glad to help out an old friend and all that. Went well last time, but it could have gone differently, from what my men told me. What's to say next time won't be so simple."

I let him do some more drinking, signalling for another beer when the time seemed right.

"How much is it worth, this job of yours," he asked, curiosity finally getting the better of him. Or was it simple greed?

"Two hundred. Just for you." Strehle didn't answer. Instead, he got up and went to the door marked *Toiletten*.

"Bit premature, don't you think?" he said on his return, pointing to the glass of schnapps I'd set next to a fresh beer.

"I need you for two days. We're talking about hands-off, static observation. Just you and me, no stress, no Russians."

"Two days? I'd have to pull a sickie ..." He sank the schnapps into the beer. "Call it three tiles and you're on."

"You forget to mention the bit about the job being in West Berlin!" Strehle hissed on Monday morning. We were crouched at the foot of the border wall, a few metres down from Wollankstrasse S-Bahn station.

Strehle had been very good, hadn't complained until the scout left us at the door in the border wall. But now we were in forward territory, West Berlin just a few metres away.

"I'm not West confirmed!" he added.

"Are you a flight risk?" I teased.

"No family to leave behind, not politically reliable. Why would they trust me in the West?"

"Relax. We go home again tomorrow and nobody will be any the wiser. Call it an experience."

We waited for the down train, then crawled up the embankment and crossed the tracks. The platform manager saw us coming but looked the other way. The wind must have changed because she continued to face the other way until the next S-Bahn arrived and we merged with the passengers leaving the station.

I led the way down the stairs and onto the street outside, maintaining awareness of Strehle the whole time.

He hesitated at the edge of the road, peering at the enamel sign *Fin du secteur Français*. I turned around and watched as he took a deep breath and slowly stepped off the kerb and into West Berlin. The commuters around us tutted and shifted around the obstruction, going on their way to the bus stop.

"Come on, you can think about it later." I tapped him on the shoulder and with a start he jerked into motion, following me as I walked around the corner.

We went to the safe flat first, where I gave him a beer and the map of West Berlin. I showed him Riemannstrasse, where Oskar lived, and told him what we needed. He set off with a BVG ticket in his hand and I just had to hope he wouldn't give himself away with his wide-eyed wonder at this Berlin through the looking glass. Familiar, but only through the lens of television.

In real life, the wash of bright colours, the shops full of consumer products and empty of queues are a shock.

The U-Bahn can be a particular challenge for the unprepared, the homeless person in the last seat trying to stay warm and just a metre or two away, the widow in her fur coat and pearls clasping her designer handbag. That's the city they call the showcase of the West, it's never quite how us Easterners expect it to be.

60
WEST BERLIN
Wedding

I waited an hour, then followed Strehle out the door. No U-Bahn ticket for me, the major had organised a new car. I Wondered for a moment what had happened to the green Kadett, maybe the British still had it, maybe they'd already sent it back to the East on a low-loader. Wherever it was, it was well and truly burnt.

I found my new wheels, an old-style blue Escort with a souped-up engine. Listening to the engine, you couldn't tell it had a bit extra under the bonnet, but I soon learnt to keep my foot light, otherwise every traffic cop in West Berlin would have been on my tail.

I parked the Escort right at the end of Oskar's street, a fair distance away from his building, and headed up the hill towards Chamissoplatz.

Once there, I found myself a bench under the bare trees and set myself down to wait. Punks were getting pissed on Aldi beer in one corner of the park, mothers were at the other end, fussing over children, tucking them up in slings and prams. I was in the middle, enjoying a rare patch of weak sunlight and keeping an eye on whoever might enter the square.

A quarter of an hour later, Strehle came down the hill from Willibald-Alexis-Strasse. He'd taken the long way round from Oskar's street and was now making a full circuit of the square before coming through the little gate that led to the benches.

He was alone, nobody on his tail, no swift swapping of the lead shadow as Strehle took the second unexpected corner.

"You found anything?" I asked as he sat on the next bench to mine. He was just a metre away from me, but we were both looking in different directions.

"Number five. Diagonally opposite Oskar," Strehle answered. "Front door isn't locked, nor is the door to the attic. Just sticks a bit, so give it a good shove."

"See you there."

Strehle got off his perch and toddled off the way he came. I waited until he was out of sight, then waited some more. If Strehle was being followed then they didn't have eyes directly on him.

After a few more minutes, I left my bench and sauntered down the hill and into the Marheineke market hall. Multiple entrances, herds of diligent shoppers funnelling through narrow gangways; it was colourful, loud and full of smells.

I queued up at a newsagents stand and just before I was about to be served, I changed my mind and went to have a look at the fruit and veg. This was a good place to dawdle, to stop and start, change direction and take a good look around. After marvelling at the pyramids of oranges and the beds of bananas, lifting the tissue paper on the chicory and examining the lawns of lettuce, I darted along a cross-aisle, entered the market hall bar and swiftly exited through an outside door. Not sure I've ever left a pub so quickly.

There were plenty of people on the street, but nobody had followed me out. A hundred metres later, I was the only one to take a left into Riemannstrasse, where a further fifty metres took me to number five. Oskar's Ford Taunus wasn't on the street outside, but if there was any kind of pattern to his life he would be at work, delivering groceries for Kaisers.

I pushed through the heavy front door and climbed the worn wooden steps to the top floor. Past the last flats and up the final twist of the stairs where they became narrow and dark. No window to let in daylight, no lightbulb to show the way. A heavier shadow at the top of the steps betrayed the position of the door into the attic. I put my shoulder to it and gave a good shove.

Rough pine beams paced the roof and obstructed my view down the length of the house. I ducked under one, then another, then sidestepped a chimney stack, all the while heading towards the front of the loft. Daylight filtered through the yellowing newspaper and cobwebs that were pasted over the windows. One corner had been scraped free of obstruction and in the light piercing the gap, Strehle was waiting for me, a magazine open on his lap.

"What you reading?" I asked.

"Zitty. Found it on the U-Bahn." He showed me the cover, a colourful cartoon, with a red title block in the top-left corner. "Have you seen all the events? And these adverts!"

I sat on a chair next to Strehle, who continued to flick through the magazine while I peered through the gap in the newspaper covering the window.

"Lots of political cartoons in here, too," Strehle said. "I don't understand most of them, but some are very critical."

I couldn't tell whether he thought that was a good thing or not. I had a look at what he was reading. A caricature of a policeman, baton raised, threatening a naked couple in bed. One half of the couple had large breasts with oversized nipples, the other a beard through which wide lips peeked, but both had equally long hair and both were scared of the policeman and his truncheon.

"You're not on holiday," I told him. "Set yourself up by that window and watch the traffic on the street."

Strehle got up and teased apart the sheets of newspaper glued to the windows. When he was happy with his field of observation, I told him to watch out for a four-door burgundy-coloured Ford Taunus saloon and gave him the registration. When he was settled, I went to the attic door and screwed on a heavy bolt to deter unwanted visitors.

Satisfied with my work, I returned to the chairs and flicked through Strehle's magazine.

"What are we hoping to catch?" Strehle asked from the window.

I put the magazine down and looked at the back of the policeman's head. I hadn't briefed him properly, unsure how much information to let him have. Professional caution told me to keep it to a minimum. Major Blecher had ordered me to tell him nothing. My sense of self-preservation told me to tell him as little as possible.

Strehle had been passed to me second-hand—a few months ago another contact had given me the material I'd needed to pressure him into doing a first job for me. If I'd come by the policeman so easily, there was a good chance that he was also being handled by another colleague in the Ministry.

But, we had an understanding, Strehle and I. He didn't ask too many questions and he did good work—so far, he'd not let me down. Very few people I could say that about.

"We're working off the books." I ignored Strehle's snort. "The subject, codename Oskar, is a citizen of West Berlin. He makes irregular journeys into the territory of the GDR."

"The woods last week? the one meeting the biker?"

"We have his place wired and I've been tailing him here in West Berlin. But I was warned off by the Russians." I didn't bother mentioning the British, I don't like to be the cause of needless worry.

Strehle glanced away from the window and gave a low whistle. His eyes went back to the window and continued his constant sweep of the street below.

There was silence for a minute or two.

"You like to live dangerously, don't you?" he stated. "I don't mind, but I wish you'd tell me *before* you dragged me into these things."

The policeman had a point.

61
WEST BERLIN
Kreuzberg

We swapped places at the window regularly. Strehle went out for supplies, a few beers and a bottle of schnapps. I watched as he walked down the street, discreetly checking the interior of each vehicle as he went.

Ten minutes later, I watched him return on the opposite side of the road.

"Nothing obvious," he reported when I let him into the attic.

I stayed by the window, accepting a beer when it came my way. Strehle started looking at his magazine again, examining the personal ads with great interest.

Oskar arrived shortly after 1600 hours. I called Strehle to the window and we both watched as the Ford cruised down the street, looking for a gap in the row of 2CVs, Beetles, Golfs and small Fiats. He found one and neatly parallel parked into place, then walked back to his tenement block and through the doors.

"Didn't even glance around," observed Strehle. "Either he's very cool or he's an innocent who's fallen into our world by mistake."

I didn't answer, I was too busy watching a silver Fiesta. It had trailed Oskar down the street and continued on when Oskar parked. Now it had stopped at the junction at the other end of the road and a man was getting out. Medium height, he wore a dark-grey flat cap pulled low over his eyes, a bulky grey anorak and blue jeans. He crossed to our side of the street and out of sight.

"Do any of these windows open? Come on, we have to open a window so we can see out!"

Strehle stood up and started pushing at one of the windows, but they were all painted shut.

"Get down there—down to the street," I ordered. "Grey anorak, dark-grey cap, jeans—find out where he goes!"

The policeman ran across the attic, pulled the door open and crashed down the stairs. I remained at the window, watching for any other movements. For the moment, the street was empty.

Strehle returned, his breathing still laboured. "Nobody there," he reported.

"How long before you got to the outside door?"

"Twenty, maybe thirty seconds." I pushed my face to the pane of glass again, so that I could see the junction where the car had let out the passenger. At least fifty metres, more like sixty.

"He probably entered a building on this side of the street, somewhere between here and the junction down there," I decided.

"You think he was part of a team watching Oskar?"

"We'll have to find out."

62
WEST BERLIN
Kreuzberg

Twenty minutes later, Oskar left his building. He turned left, walking in the direction of the shops.

"You're on again," I told Strehle, but he was already on the other side of the heavy chimney stack, half-way to the door.

"Confirmed," he gasped on return, still breathing heavily from climbing five flights of stairs.

Strehle hadn't tailed Oskar and his shadow, we were being too cautious for that. But he had waited in a doorway a block or two further down the street. When Oskar returned with a bag of shopping, Strehle had housed the shadow.

"His tail went into a tenement four doors along," he reported.

"Any idea who he might be, where he's from?"

"He didn't have a copy of Pravda under his arm if that's what you're asking. Nor the London Times or the Herald Tribune."

Fair point. But sometimes you take a guess and you're lucky. Didn't look like Strehle was prepared to take that guess. I sent him off to sit in the car further down the street where he could keep an eye on the building where Oskar's other shadow was hiding out. I stayed by the window, beer in hand, one eye on Oskar's front door, the other on our blue Escort at the end of the street.

★

While I was waiting and watching, I popped another beer and had myself a bit of quiet thinking time.

Oskar was being watched. He'd been followed home from work and there was an observation point opposite his building. If the surveillance we'd spotted today had anything to do with me being picked up last week then Oskar's tail must be Soviet or British.

It was still too early to start ruling out other agencies, I told myself, mentally listing the usual suspects: West Berlin police and *Verfassungsschutz*. The American or British Occupation forces.

And let's not forget our own side—Oskar made frequent trips to the GDR and he didn't follow the rules when he was over there. I may not be the only one in the Firm to have taken note of his illegal stops in the small woodland. Perhaps another part of the Stasi had become aware of Oskar, in which case they would have requested surveillance support from Blecher's parish, Main Department VIII.

It wasn't unheard of for different parts of the Ministry, even different parts of the same department to be working the same subject at the same time. Normally the problem would show up in the files, but there wasn't any paperwork for this case.

A final thought, totally out there, yet on consideration, not quite impossible: what if the other watchers were also working for Major Blecher? My brainwork was interrupted by movement in the middle of the street. I shifted my gaze and watched the silver Fiesta pause to pick up the guy in the grey anorak, then drive past my blue Escort. A quick glance back along the street to where Oskar's Taunus was still parked, good, Oskar hadn't made a move while I was daydreaming. Looked like the observation was having a shift change.

I watched our Escort pull out and follow the Fiesta around the corner. Strehle was on the case, he'd report back in good time. Meanwhile, I had Oskar's front door to keep an eye on.

★

It was already dark by the time Strehle returned.

A gas lamp lit the street outside Oskar's house, I was confident I'd recognise our subject if he stepped outside, but it was too dim for me to get a reliable description of other people going in and out of his block, not to mention pedestrians passing on by.

I slid the bolt back to let Strehle in.

"In Reinickendorf," he told me, pulling the map out of his pocket. We moved further back from the window and I shone a torch on the floor while he unfolded the street plan, looking for the place he'd followed the silver Fiesta to. "Up in the French sector—saw a French army foot patrol and some armoured cars ... near Tegel airport ... here it was." He tapped a finger on a road just north of where the motorway dives under the runway of Tegel airport.

I squinted at the map. "Auguste-Viktoria-Allee?"

Strehle trailed his finger along the length of the road, then pointed at a block about half-way.

"Describe it to me," I said.

"Wide road, two lanes each direction, trees down the middle. Light industry at this end, new build flats down here. Mix of 1930s and modern flats in the middle. Big church ..."

It sounded familiar, the location markers fitted. After my meeting with Pozdniakov I'd been driven home. They'd been quick about it, not giving me much chance to take stock of my surroundings.

But I had seen a little and I'd been able to hear. We'd been close to the airport, not directly under the flight path, but not far away either. The groan of traffic on the motorway to the west had been punctuated by the intermittent roar of planes to the south. The geography fitted.

"Where did they go?" I asked.

"Some kind of compound. High brick wall, big gate."

That was where I'd been taken to meet the Russian captain. Oskar's shadows were KGB.

63
WEST BERLIN
Kreuzberg

I showed Strehle the first rendezvous on the map, then the back-up. Once he'd left the building I tidied up—removing as many traces of our temporary occupation as I could. By the time I'd finished the only signs of our presence were two old chairs stacked against the far wall and fresh screw holes in the door where I'd removed the bolt.

Out on the street, I stayed close to the buildings, hopefully out of sight of the KGB watchers a few houses further on. I beetled to the corner, took another couple of turns, disposed of Strehle's listings magazine in a litter bin then entered the courtyard behind a random tenement to throw the bolt into a wheelie bin.

At Gneisenaustrasse U-Bahn station I let a train leave in each direction, then got on the next service heading west—but only after waiting for the red lights to flash and the buzzer to sound.

The doors clamped shut, catching the tail of my jacket. The train hummed off, almost immediately throwing itself into a sharp curve, the next stop was Mehringdamm and I played with the idea of changing trains: just skip across the platform and I could be at Friedrichstrasse station in four stops. I'd step off the train, walk up the steps to the tunnel that led to the underground S-Bahn platform and knock on the steel door that none of the commuters ever noticed, a packet of L&M

cigarettes in my breast pocket, lid torn: the signal to let me enter.

I'd be home. But being home wouldn't help. Schöneiche landfill awaited, or if I chose to continue this mission, Captain or Major or whatever he was Pozdniakov could reach me whichever side of the Wall I was on.

I let Mehringdamm station slip behind and got off at Möckernbrücke, moving with the crowds across the glassed-in pedestrian bridge to the U1 line on the other side of the canal. At the far end I slowed down, allowing the streams of passengers around me to thin and dry up.

When I heard a train rumble in overhead, I ran up the steps to the eastbound platform and jumped aboard.

Strehle and I made the first rendezvous, both of us satisfied we hadn't grown any tails. We ended up in a grimy bar in the last corner of Kreuzberg, close enough to throw a beer bottle over the Wall.

"Are we finished over here?" Strehle asked over the harsh shouting that some of the safety pin-pierced in the bar might call music. To me it was just noise, but that was fine. The more noise, the less chance we had of being overheard.

"For the time being, yes," I answered. "I've got what I needed ..."

"Tell me if you want any help with putting it all together." Strehle sank his beer and clicked the bottle back onto the sticky table.

It was a tempting offer because I had no clue what to do with all the jagged shards of information I'd gathered over the last six weeks. Strehle and I were on the same wavelength and he was one of the few people I knew who wasn't determined to see me back on the rubbish heap.

"Not much to tell," I shouted into his ear. He had his hand over the other ear, trying to keep out the sound of a thudding drum machine and the screaming of a punkette on the little stage in the corner.

"Wait!" I read his lips as he held his palm up. I waited while he fought his way through to the bar, reaching in between a sixteen-year-old made up to look like she'd been dead for twenty years and a young lad trying to impress her with his *irokese* cockscomb of purple-dyed hair.

Strehle returned with four bottles, the necks clasped between the fingers of his left hand. He took a bottle, hung the crown cap over the edge of the scarred table and brought the base of his hand down on top. The bottle dropped a few centimetres as the cap sprung off into the dark. I took the beer and drank as he opened the second bottle in the same way.

"Puzzle?" he prompted after he'd had a few pulls from his beer.

I looked Strehle in the eyes. They were beginning to redden but were still clear enough. He already had more than enough compromising material on me—one word from him, directed in the right ear, and I'd never see daylight again. I had little to lose from talking to him and something to gain.

"Oskar is being run by the British," my head was next to Strehle's, my mouth just a centimetre or two from his ear. "He's also in operational contact with the Big Brothers-"

"The man on the motorbike?" Strehle broke in.

I nodded. The man on the motorbike who had disappeared into the Soviet base after Oskar had handed over the material.

"And he's under observation by the Russians, here in West Berlin?" Strehle thought he'd completed the short list of my puzzle pieces and sat back, rewarding himself with a satisfied pull of beer.

But I wasn't quite finished. I leant forward again and Strehle moved his head closer.

"I was interrogated by the British but I got away, then I was picked up by the KGB."

"Woah, you were interrogated by the British, *and you got away*?" I nodded while Strehle shook his head again. My story was barely credible. At the time, my escape from the cellar had felt very real, but since then I'd begun having doubts. I had questions: Did they let me escape? Why hold me in a cellar and not on some army base? Was it really the British?

"Tell me about the KGB." Strehle had already moved onto the next point.

"Not much to say. They wanted to know what I was up to, gave me a warning and took me home."

Strehle opened the next bottle of beer. Same way as the last ones, cap on edge of table, knock the top. "All because of Oskar?" he said. More statement than question. "The Stasi, the British military, the KGB are all interested in Oskar? And you thought it would be fun to drag me over to West Berlin and set me up as a target?"

I watched Strehle take a deep draught of his beer. He put the bottle back on the table and stood up. I don't know whether what he said next was out loud or whether he just mimed the words.

Either way, the meaning was clear.

"Fuck you!"

64
WEST BERLIN
Wedding

I waited for Strehle back at the safe flat in Wedding. Trapped in this island of a half-city, he had to turn up sooner or later. He couldn't get home, the Wall was in the way and once the bars closed, there was nowhere else for him to go.

The doorbell woke me shortly after three in the morning. I let Strehle in, watching his entry in silence. He walked slowly and deliberately, as if he had to think about each movement before he made it, but his voice was steady.

"Oskar is the cut-out between the Brits and some Soviet based in Wünsdorf. Someone with access to intelligence that NATO wants," he announced as soon as I had the flat door shut.

I poured a schnapps and gave him the glass. He took it and held it up, half-way between us.

"Fuck you!" he toasted, then downed the alcohol. "And your KGB friend is onto Oskar, which is why they're watching him. They're playing the long game, who knows why. They could have picked him up any time he crossed the border. But they didn't. They're lying in wait, biding their time. Ours not to reason why."

I went back to the sofa and poured myself a shot and drank it, listening to what Strehle had to say.

"I have two questions. How did you get away from the British and why is your Stasi boss so interested in Oskar?"

"I've got the same questions," I told him.

But he wasn't listening. He thumped over to the bottle and gave himself another measure. "Do you always have this much bad luck with your bosses? Listen to me, if your boss tells you to do something, then you do it. But you do it by the book. That's how it works." He waited a moment, giving me a chance to acknowledge what he was saying. "Don't get involved in any of this hush-hush, secret-secret shit. You only get into trouble and then you get me in trouble." He knocked back the glass of schnapps and, without undressing, lay down on the bed in the next room, pulling the covers over himself.

Wisdom can sometimes be found in a bottle, but it's not always very useful.

I sat with my schnapps for another couple of hours, then packed our things before turfing Strehle out of bed. He wasn't happy about it, but he cheered up when I told him we were going home.

We got to Wollankstrasse station well before sun-up and waited until the platform manager gave us the nod before loping across the tracks and down the embankment to the Wall below.

I let Strehle make his own way back to Königs Wusterhausen and, desperate as I was to get back to my flat for a long sleep, I had a report to make first.

I arrived at the safe flat in Köpenick and got into position at the window in time to watch Major Blecher pick his way across the car-park below. He came alone, not looking around, his steps unhurried.

A couple of minutes later he was letting himself into the flat. He joined me at the window. We stood side by side, looking out over the parked cars and the kindergarten below.

"Well? What have you got to report?" he asked.

"Oskar is subject to continual surveillance in the

independent political entity of West Berlin."

"By whom?"

"Pozdniakov," I replied. I told him that Oskar was the cut-out between an as-yet unidentified Soviet officer based in Wünsdorf and the British Army in West Berlin.

Superior officers don't like conjecture. They like facts. And if all you have to offer are theories, then the way to an easy life lies in enhancing your theories and guesswork into something that looks like a fact or two. Make verbal reports sound definite, if necessary you can revise it all later, they never remember the exact details anyway.

Blecher licked his lips and started pacing the room, his hands behind his back. He liked what he'd heard, was savouring the feeling of being one step closer to solving the whole Oskar case.

"And?" he'd come to a stop by the dining table, hands still joined behind his back, chest puffed out. Ready to hear about all the material he could use. The kind of material I didn't have.

"And what, Comrade Major?" I asked, squashing my face into as innocent a look as I could manage at short notice.

"What else? Dammit, you were there for twenty-four hours, what else have you got for me?" Typical VIII, wanting immediate results. When other departments need a suspect tailed or a flat searched, they drop HA VIII a line, who come and do the job and pass on the reports. It makes them feel superior because they're doing something other departments don't, they feel like they're providing results because they come in at the sharp end of an investigation. But they don't appreciate all the preparations, the basic sleuthing and legwork that can, in some cases, take years. All they know is that they provide their expertise and pretty soon after that the case is wrapped up.

The captain was expecting me to say something, so I did. Even though I knew I had nothing he'd want to hear.

"It's a sensitive operation, Comrade Captain and so far I have been unable to identify Pozdniakov's interest-"

"Don't give me all that malarkey! How long have you been on this case? Six weeks, two months? And what do you have to show for your jollies to the Capitalist West? Spending hard currency we can't afford, yet all you find to bring back is the name of a Russian captain who may or may not be involved!" Blecher continued for a while in that vein.

All he required me to do was to stand there and look like I was paying attention. No need to listen, I knew what he was saying: he wasn't happy about the slow progress and it was all my fault and if there were no progress by this afternoon or tomorrow or whatever random date he came up with then I'd be sent back to Schöneiche.

"*Jawohl, Genosse Major*," I snapped out when it seemed like Blecher was finally winding down.

65
BERLIN KÖPENICK

Blecher wanted immediate results. He wanted to hear something juicy about Pozdniakov, something he could take upstairs in the hope of getting a pat on the head, a medal and a promotion.

Did I already mention that I wasn't convinced by his strategy? When the time came for him to execute his ill-advised plans, I was going to head straight back to Schöneiche and threaten, cajole and bribe every single colleague on the landfill until they were prepared to swear blind that I hadn't left the dump in the last six weeks.

I admit, it's not exactly a waterproof plan, but that was what was going through my head as I finally climbed the stairs in my block of flats, wanting only my bed. I needed to find a way of putting some distance between myself and Blecher's murky ambitions, I hoped I'd have some better ideas after a lie-down.

When I put the key in the door to my flat and opened up, a KGB major was sitting in my armchair.

Coming home to find the KGB have made themselves comfortable in my living room has never been an ambition of mine. In fact, the sight of the officer in my armchair brought on a nasty bout of deja-vu.

Do I need to tell you the major's name? I'll give you a clue: last time I saw him, he was sitting in the shadows, wearing an artillery captain's uniform. This morning, he was sitting in a beam of sunlight, his glass eye gleaming at me.

"Come in, Comrade Second Lieutenant," Pozdniakov spoke in German, he gave me a friendly wave, a bit like the Comrade General Secretary Erich Honecker does—good-natured yet slightly patronising. I came in and closed the flat door behind me then crossed the vestibule and stood by the living room door.

As far as I could see, everything was as it should be: overflowing ashtrays, empty beer bottles, half-empty vodka and schnapps bottles.

"Comrade Reim," Pozdniakov had stopped waving and was fixing me with his good eye. His falsie focussed on the grey screen of the television in the corner. "I have a problem, Reim, and I think you know what he's called."

I remained by the door. I couldn't wait to hear the punchline.

"You and I have already had a chat. I think we understand each other, don't we?" Half of Pozdniakov's mouth curled up in a smile, it didn't make him any prettier. "But how much is this understanding between the two of us worth if you have an ambitious major of the MfS behind you, prodding you on?"

Slightly disconcerting, hearing Pozdniakov use exactly the same adjective to describe Blecher, the one that had been going through my head not five minutes since.

"So now you're here," Pozdniakov held up an index finger. "Major Blecher on one side." Another index finger was held up, "and Major Pozdniakov on the other. You're piggie in the middle. I think it's fair to say it's in your interest to find a solution to this problem, don't you agree?"

For all his theatrics, the KGB major was talking sense. But I wasn't sure I was going to enjoy hearing his idea of a solution to the problem.

"How do you know I'm going to deal with things the way that you'd want?" It was the first thing I'd said to him.

"Because of who you are." Pozdniakov laughed. He put his head back and gave a good chuckle, like a baby being burped.

"You're different. I think I can work with you—that's the only reason you're still alive." He let that sink in for a moment or two, then he carried on, mouth still crimped into half a smile. "Your previous superior officer ..." he pretended to think, finger tapping his temple, "Captain Fröhlich, that was his name, no?" It was obvious that Pozdniakov knew damn well what my previous Boss was called, he just wanted me to acknowledge his ability to gather intelligence.

I nodded, if only to get the conversation flowing again.

"So, this Fröhlich had you in a position not so very different from the one you're in now—am I right? OK, perhaps quite different, but still, not too dissimilar. You showed ability, flexibility, ingenuity even. I could use a contact like you in the MfS."

"You know I'm in the doghouse?" Stupid question. If Pozdniakov knew about my previous Boss, he'd know I was on a punishment assignment pending judgement being handed down by Berlin Centre.

"That can change. When we're finished, you'll be able to choose what you want to do, where you want to go, which department. Providing you make the right decision and pass a couple of little tests."

Choose my own career path, that sounded tempting. I was thinking of the smallest, quietest county office in the furthest corner of the Republic. Somehow I doubted it would be that easy. The KGB, Russian big brother to the Stasi, called the shots—if they wanted me moved away from Schöneiche, they could make it happen with a phone call. But I couldn't imagine Pozdniakov going to even that much trouble unless he thought there would be something for him in return. I'd be of little use to him in a quiet, country office.

There was also the small matter of what the Russian had called little tests. That bothered me too. "Tests?"

"First of all, I want to know how far you've got with your investigation into Oskar." He waved again, this time towards a chair. I took the hint.

"Subject Oskar, real name Schraber Olli," I began. "West Berlin-based delivery driver for a West German supermarket. At irregular intervals he drives a West Berlin refuse truck to the Schöneiche landfill in the Potsdam district. Whenever that happens he does a brush past with someone who in turn has access to the Soviet Army base in Wünsdorf." I paused to see how I was doing. The Russian was nodding along, paying attention, but not too much. "There's some kind of debrief when he returns to West Berlin, in a villa in Grunewald. Presumably British Army intelligence." That was pretty much all I knew. Weeks of work, summed up in a few sentences.

"A debriefing you say? Your Oskar is debriefed?" Pozdniakov leaned forward, steepling his fingers and leaning his chin on them.

"That seems to be what happens, at least, that's what happened the night we first met." I wasn't telling Pozdniakov anything I hadn't already done when he interrogated me in West Berlin last week, but he seemed satisfied enough.

"Anything you've missed out?" he prompted.

"Oskar is under continuous observation. I'm guessing by your lot?"

The officer nodded. It wasn't exactly an admission, but I could take it that way if I chose to.

He stood up, interview over. The only thing remaining to be seen was whether he'd tell me about the second test right now or whether I'd be getting the details in the post.

"You mentioned two tests," I said. "I presume I've just passed the first test, telling you everything I know about Oskar? So what about the second?"

"Major Blecher," the Russian said as he got up from my armchair. "Venal, ambitious and stupid. Not a wholesome combination in any man, but unforgivable in a Chekist."

Pozdniakov was passing me now, he filled the vestibule with his presence. One hand was on the handle of the flat door, one eye was on me. I looked back into that eye, trying not to let my own eyes slide off towards the falsie. The glass eye that may or may not have been made from an eye scooped from a conscript's face.

"Deal with Blecher," Pozdniakov said. "I can't help you while he's interfering."

66
BERLIN FRIEDRICHSHAIN

I shut and locked the flat door behind Pozdniakov then quickly crossed to the window and looked down to the street below. He appeared at the front door and went down the steps, a grey raincoat over his uniform jacket, his officer's cap in the brown leather bag he was carrying. I'd expected a car to be waiting, but he walked off down the road, heading for the junction that would take him to to the S-Bahn.

I poured myself a vodka. Then one more. After I'd finished with that, I went to bed.

But I couldn't sleep.

Pozdniakov's orders—and he'd left me in no doubt they were orders—were to neutralise Major Blecher. These new orders were pretty much the converse of those I'd received from my handler Blecher, who wanted me to come up with the proof needed to discredit Pozdniakov.

But, unlike Blecher, Pozdniakov inspired respect. Pozdniakov was never reduced to making empty threats in order to maintain discipline. Pozdniakov was twice the officer Blecher would ever be.

And me? I wanted only to survive and if I had to sell my allegiance in the process, then that was fine by me.

After coming to some sort of a decision I drifted off to sleep, dozing fitfully until high pitched voices roused me. I lay still for a moment, wondering why I could hear children, before my brain ratcheted into gear and I realised the sounds were coming from the stairwell outside the flat.

I turned on my side and reached for the travel alarm clock folded into its pouch, flipping it open and focussing on the dial. It was after three in the afternoon.

With a groan I sat up, swung my feet out of bed and, ignoring the pounding in my head, padded out to the shower.

Ten minutes under the cold water cleared the pipes and, even though I didn't leap out of the shower cubicle like Rudolf Nureyev, I did at least feel a lot more awake.

Ignoring the half-full bottles of vodka and schnapps, I fished a hard piece of dried sausage from the fridge and cut a couple of slices from the even harder heel of grey bread. A smear of butter was all I had left in the packet and the plum spread was mouldy. But all together, a fine breakfast. More than enough to set me up for the afternoon ahead.

While I exercised my jaw on the bread and sausage, I focussed on the threads of a plan that were waving around between my ears. I nodded to myself. Could work, could be doable.

I pushed the plate away and got up to fetch a map, coming back with a medium-scale district map of Potsdam. I didn't have anything larger-scale, didn't even have access to anything more detailed. But this one would serve its purpose.

With my finger, I traced the border between West Berlin and the GDR. I didn't waste any time looking at the line dividing the city—the defences there were tighter than the calculations for a five-year plan.

I was looking for a stretch of border with woods on both sides. My finger brushed past the southern edges of West Berlin until it reached the area around the motorway border crossing at Drewitz.

Just south of there was the motorway bridge over the Teltow Canal, where the border crossing point for bulk transport barges was serviced by a little lane coming from Kleinmachnow.

It was a strange area, a finger of West Berlin crooked out from the city's southern flank, and the Wall took a shortcut between the end of that finger and the rest of West Berlin. I crossed the room to the bag I'd brought back from West Berlin and pulled out the West Berlin map. Flattening it out on the table, I found the area I was looking for. Albrechtsteerofen was the name of the finger of land.

The border fortifications weren't shown on this map, but the course of an abandoned stretch of motorway was marked in a lighter shade and I knew the final fences were positioned a few metres to the east of this.

But, looking at the map, I could see the problems with this area—there was only one route in and out, and access would be restricted. That meant any movements in the area would be logged.

My finger carried on around the edge of West Berlin in a clockwise direction, past the lakes around Potsdam. Nothing doing here, too many restricted areas, too many fences, walls and bodies of water. I ignored the next few kilometres, opposite the British military airport, went past Staaken and onto the nested enclaves and exclaves around Eiskeller.

This was another curious area. If you were there on the ground you'd find it impossible to locate the border—it follows one side of a ditch, returns on the other, goes around a field and doubles back on itself. For that reason the fences had been erected up to 800 metres before the actual border. That made it unsuitable for my purposes.

Just around the corner from Eiskeller, the border made a beeline for the River Havel, due east-south-east. The whole sector was remote and heavily wooded, with no nearby dwellings on the West Berlin side.

I'd found what I needed.

67
BERLIN MARZAHN

I had two phone calls to make that afternoon, my next steps would depend on how quickly I could get a response.

A trip on the S-Bahn, followed by a tram ride and a short walk led me to a random phone box in Marzahn. I dialled the Berlin number that Pozdniakov had given me and waited to be connected. After a couple of rings, a click and a beep told me I could talk to an answer machine. I recited the agreed code-name and asked for a meeting.

After that, a bus ride, a few stops on the S-Bahn and another stop on the U-Bahn, then another walk. My second phone call was to Major Blecher, requesting permission for another crossing into West Berlin.

The Major agreed to my request but limited my stay in the West to twenty-four hours. That suited me—what I needed to do shouldn't take that long.

I was picked up in Pankow shortly before 2000 hours and taken to the Wollankstrasse conspirative crossing. As I crouched in the shadow of the Wall, waiting to make my way to the station, I could see the lights from the top floors of the apartment blocks on the other side of the tracks, in West Berlin. If anyone looked closely, they might see the shadow that was me, huddled between Wall and railway embankment. Was this another possibility? I thought about it while I waited for the next down train to whistle through. This place could work, but it would leave too many untidy ends. I filed it away for future reference and loped along the edge of the embankment, ready to head up and over the tracks to West Berlin.

I picked up supplies on the way to the safe flat—I would have preferred to save my hard currency by bringing the beer and cigarettes with me, but security concerns required the consumption of purely Western brands.

Once at the flat, I sat and watched television. I tuned in to the first channel of *DDR Fernsehen*. Call it *Heimweh* if you wish—even if I was only five or six kilometres from home.

I was up at first light to go in search of the blue Escort. Since I'd last been here it had been cleaned up and filled with petrol, somebody was taking care of it. I struggled through the morning traffic to Spandau, then headed north and found a parking space in a residential street.

I walked to the hospital, slowing down once I got close. I lit a cigarette, using the pause to take a look around. There was no car park as such, but a row of bikes by the main entrance had their front wheels moored to a rack. I walked along the row, spotting what I was after—a bike in my size, decent tyres and a cheap chain. The lock was a combination type, I didn't even need to get my picks out, I just had to put it under tension while I turned the numbered discs.

When the lock gave a little, I moved on to the next disc. Within fifteen seconds I had the bike free and without looking around, I mounted and headed off. Traffic soon thinned and, within a couple of kilometres, I had the road to myself, cycling through the Spandau Forest towards the border.

It was a dull day, the air cool but close under the serried conifers. But I wasn't here to talk about the weather, I had some serious work to do.

Five kilometres later I stopped at a big white sign, *End of British Sector*. The notice was redundant—a few metres beyond, the border wall blocked any further progress. To my right, a path dived between the straight stems of the pine trees and I followed the sandy track for a few metres before checking my position on the West Berlin street map. I was in the right place, my work could begin.

I pulled a dark baseball cap low over my eyes and headed along the track until the way forward was cut off by the Wall again. Another track branched off to the right, following the course of the border, staying on the West Berlin side. Vehicle tyre tracks could be seen in the soft sand.

It was hard going on the bike and I had to get off and push much of the time. My view to the left was obstructed by the whitewashed flanks of the Wall, but that was fine—right now I was more interested in the topography to my right. The track along the border alternately climbed shallow banks then dived into sand-ridden depressions, but whatever the shape of the land, the whitewashed concrete barrier remained a constant companion.

It was nearly midday when I found what I was looking for. The Wall and the path I was following mounted the flank of a low hill, the summit lying just to the south. A steel-lined crack in the Wall traced a low, square door, sixty centimetres by eighty—just like the one near Wollankstrasse that I'd been using so often these last few weeks. The door allowed Border Scouts access to the forward territory to check for any damage to the border defences.

I didn't waste any time admiring it but continued along my way until I found a path that headed off to my right, southwards and away from the border. I took the path, then doubled back, abandoning the bike and heading up the slope of the hill.

When I neared the crest, I dropped to my stomach and slowly crawled northwards until I was in sight of the border again. From here, I could see over the top of the Wall, right into the security strip. It was all laid out before me: border wall, sand strip, signal-fence and floodlights. A few metres further back was the patrol road, made of perforated concrete slabs. On the other side of that, the first fence held back the forests of Brandenburg.

To my left, a BT11 watchtower towered over the strip, the observation platform about level with where I lay between the trees. I fetched my binoculars and checked the windows for any signs of life, but the tower was empty. A scan along the border wall and the strip behind but, other than the door in the Wall, I couldn't see any other infrastructure.

This was the place.

68
WEST BERLIN
Spandau

I spent the rest of the afternoon on my belly in the sand, timing the foot patrols and watching the *Stoffhund* open-top Trabants go by. This stretch of the border bulged a little to the south, which would restrict the guards' vision along the security strip.

At 1600 hours I crept backwards until the border was no longer in sight, then went down the slope and retrieved the bike. Thirty minutes later, I was back in Spandau.

I locked the bike up where I'd found it and took the Ford back to Wedding. Two hours after that, I was in a phone box, reporting my return to East Berlin.

"I've made a lot of progress, I need to speak to you," I told Major Blecher. There was silence at the end of the line for nearly a minute, then the major spoke:

"Meet me in Pankow in an hour." I didn't get a chance to reply, he'd already hung up.

I caught a variety of trams, buses and S-Bahn trains until I was in a part of the city that I'd never been to before, then phoned the number Pozdniakov had given me. This time a real person answered. She spoke in German, but with a heavy Slavic accent.

"*Ja, bitte schön?*"

"Burattino here. Do you have a message for me?"

There was a click in the line and I thought I'd lost the

connection, then she came back. "Museum of Natural History, tomorrow at 0605 hours. Follow the marks from the main entrance."

Another click, this time more pronounced, followed by the dialling tone.

I'd received my message.

69
BERLIN PANKOW

After all the trailing around Berlin I was late for my appointment with Major Blecher. It bothered him more than it bothered me, but once he'd got over himself I gave him the good news.

"Oskar has the information we need, he's asked for a meet," I told him.

Blecher, who'd been fussing with his heavy coat, pulling it tighter around him to keep out the damp chill, spun round and eyed me. "What's he got?" he demanded.

"He's willing to unpack—he'll give us the whole story. He told me he's working for the Americans and that Pozdniakov is about to defect. The Americans promised him the earth, but so far all they've given him are threats and a few Deutsche Marks. He's not happy."

I had Blecher's full attention now, he'd stopped fiddling, the only movement came from his eyes. "Can he prove Pozdniakov wants to defect? I need to talk to him.".

I congratulated myself. Blecher's need for glory meant he wanted to be involved in debriefing Oskar. But I wasn't quite finished yet.

"He'll only talk to a senior officer. He said he wants to meet, quote: *Someone with a bit of clout, somebody clever enough to understand what this is worth*. He didn't want to speak to us." Blecher's eyes narrowed in displeasure, and I let him digest it for a moment or two before delivering the punchline. "He's scared of Pozdniakov. I told him you were the only one who can protect him. Now he wants to talk to you. Alone."

Blecher tilted his head back, stroking his top lip in an attempt to hide his smile. Then his shoulders hunched and his eyes opened wider.

"Where? Where does he want to meet?"

"Neutral territory. He doesn't want to meet in West Berlin, thinks the Americans are watching his every move. Can't meet over here, he's afraid of the Stasi ..." We both chuckled at the silliness of that. "He wants to meet directly on the border."

Blecher's left eyelid began to flutter a little.

"There's a place in the forest, near Hennigsdorf," I told him. "I've used it in the past for operations like this. There's a protocol, the border troops look the other way while we meet in the restricted zone. The arrangement is good for half an hour, that should be enough for a first meet." I watched Blecher for a moment, he was mopping the back of his neck, eyelid still quivering.

"He'll bring copies of the correspondence between Pozdniakov and the Americans," I added, as a sweetener.

This was more than Blecher had ever dreamed of, how could he say no?

I spent the next couple of hours briefing the major. It would probably be his first time in the field since basic military service, but I pretended not to notice how nervous he was.

From my bag I pulled a bundle of spanners, carefully wiped down and wrapped in a new piece of material. Next out were the West Berlin street map, an East German map of Potsdam district and a roll of wallpaper liner. I started with the West Berlin map, showing him Spandau.

"This is where he'll be coming from, he'll wait for you at this point." I unrolled the wallpaper liner and drew the shape of the border—three lines, one for each layer of the defences and a heavy line for the patrol road in the middle. "There's a BT11 watchtower here," a circle on the wallpaper. "But you don't need to worry, it won't be manned at night. If you see anyone in there, it'll be a comrade, making sure you're safe."

Blecher gave me a sidelong look, but I nodded reassuringly, before going back to the maps.

"There's a scout gate in the wall at this point," Another mark on the map, "it'll be left unlocked to allow Oskar to enter the security strip. Once you get the signal you come out of the forest just here." I indicated a position a hundred metres from the watchtower where the curve of the border put the edge of the forest just out of sight of the tower. "Undo the bottom panel of the fence with the 19 and 22mm ring spanners—just open it up and put it in the sand. Don't lean it against the fence, it might make a noise."

The major nodded, his eyes following every move of the pen in my hand.

"Climb through the hole in the fence and go as far as the signal fence. Once Oskar sees you there, he'll come through the gate and meet you on the other side. There's a 17mm spanner here, just in case you need to open up the signal fence. If you have to do that then only undo the bottom panel, the signal wires down there will be turned off, but the ones at the top of the fence will still be live, so don't go near them or you'll have to explain the operation to the whole Border Regiment."

Blecher drank in the information I gave him, now and again cross referencing the rough map I was drawing with the map of West Berlin.

"Oskar will bring a branch with him and so should you. When you've finished your meeting, return the way you came, using the branch to brush out your footprints in the sand strip. Have you got all of that?"

"You mentioned a signal? Oskar's going to signal me?"

"When you arrive, use a green filter on a torch. Flash twice, short and sharp. Oskar will reply with three flashes from a red torch. Any other colours, any other sequence and you abort."

"Green, twice short. Red, three times." Blecher repeated. "OK, what about approach routes?"

"Dress in civilian clothes. Take a vehicle and drive around the Berliner Ring to Hennigsdorf. Leave the car here, at the start of this lane: Oberjägerweg in Niederneuendorf. You'll be checked at least once by police or border troops in this area and for operational reasons they won't know about the mission. Just show them your MfS identity card and do the officer act." Blecher smiled at that, unaware of my sarcasm.

"These are the areas you're likely to be checked," I pointed to the northern edge of the village of Niederneuendorf, the entrance to the woods and a track that joined the Oberjägerweg with another lane that ran towards the Border Troops' barracks. "Head due south through the woods until you reach the border."

I checked my superior was still following, then continued: "At 0250, flash your signal. If there's no response, repeat at 0305 then leave after two minutes if there's no response. There's no fallback."

"What happens if there's any difficulty with controls in the hinterland?" Blecher asked after digesting all this information for a minute or two.

"Don't tell them where you are going or why, no matter who's doing the asking. Do whatever you need to do to get to the meet. I don't think I'll be able to persuade Oskar to come again."

70
BERLIN FRIEDRICHSHAIN

I woke the next morning, refreshed and in plenty of time for my appointment with Pozdniakov. Lying in bed for a few more minutes, I wondered, not for the first time, whether to scout out the Museum for Natural History before Pozdniakov turned up. I was tempted, but suspected that our meeting wouldn't actually be there, that I'd arrive only to be directed elsewhere.

I hadn't had a chance to go shopping and the bakers wouldn't be open this early, so there was no breakfast. At least I had the bag of ground coffee I'd brought back from West Berlin.

I made my way to the Museum by S-Bahn, then tram, getting off a couple of stops early so as not to arrive too soon.

At 0604 I was crossing the grassy strip at the front of the heavily classical museum building. The doors were firmly shut, the only people in sight were those hurrying to work along the road behind me. I paused at the bottom of the steps, looking for the marks the lady on the telephone had instructed me to follow.

There was nothing to be seen. Not that I was expecting a big sign: *Clandestine meeting with the KGB here* → , but a chalk mark on the facade or the steps would have been nice.

The double wooden doors were set in the middle of three porticos and I went up the steps to check the window in each of the flanking arches. No smears on the window, no scratches on the frame or the stonework below. I turned around to go back down the steps and smiled when I spotted the ticket caught in a crack in the steps.

I bent down to pick it up, pulling hard to release it from the tight joint in the stonework. It was a standard S-Bahn ticket, thin, brown cardboard, with a hole punched in the top right corner. It hadn't just fallen out of someone's pocket or been thrown away, this had been carefully eased into the gap. A gap on the right-hand edge of the steps.

Back down the steps, slowly sweep to the right of the building, keeping the old eyes open for further clues. A veteran lime tree stood at the edge of the grass and, in the trunk, about a metre from the ground, a further S-Bahn ticket had been stuck into the ridges of the bark. The ticket was at an angle, pointing towards the gap between the Museum and the next building along.

I followed the path between the buildings, coming to an enclosed vehicle park. It was quiet here, work not yet started for the day. The few lamps fastened to the walls of the surrounding buildings cast an orange glow that left deep shadows between the vans and cars.

This was more like the scene for a quiet meeting and, reassured, I peered into each shadow around the edge of the car park. I followed the walls of the surrounding buildings until I found the next ticket. It was jammed into a gap where the stucco had come away from the brickwork of the ruins of the east wing of the museum, bombed during the war and never rebuilt.

The ticket was positioned right next to a doorway, and taking the hint, I turned the handle. The door opened silently on oiled hinges and I darted inside, quickly moving to the side and pressing myself against the wall.

It was hard to see much, shafts of orange light came through the windows, slanting across the floor and far wall, but leaving the rest of the high room in darkness.

The scrape of a shoe came from the right as a figure flitted through an orange bar and back into the shadows.

"Good morning." It was Pozdniakov.

I didn't reply at once, I stayed where I was, remaining aware, wondering whether the major and I were alone.

"You needn't worry, we're the only ones here," he said, as if I'd put my thoughts into words.

He was closer now, I could make out his silhouette against the slatted light behind him.

"You asked for a meet?" he said.

"I have Major Blecher where I need him, but first I want to know more about Oskar," I replied.

Pozdniakov was still some distance away, in the darkness it was hard to tell exactly how far. There was silence while he moved towards me, no footfall to be heard as he crossed from shadow to shadow, never approaching a window, avoiding crossing any of the orange beams of light.

"*Horosho*," he said once he was within a couple of metres. "I'll tell you what you want to know about Oskar, but this cannot go any further. Even if you told anyone they wouldn't believe you, they wouldn't want to believe you—what I am about to tell you is too dangerous to believe."

I'd heard this spiel before, it was the kind spies the world over like to have. Makes them feel important. I let Pozdniakov have his awestruck silence. Let him play it the way he wanted.

"That day in Grunewald—you're sure it was Oskar you saw?"

I needed his help, so I had little choice but to play along with the smug Russian. I considered the matter: the person I'd followed that day had driven Oskar's truck to the municipal waste depot in Ruhleben and then his car to Grunewald. I'd seen him as he entered the villa, there was nothing wrong with my memory. I looked at Pozdniakov, he stared at me, willing me to question my memory.

What did he want? Was this some kind of faith thing, two

plus two equals five? Did I need to prove I had the necessary discipline to rearrange my memory to suit the KGB's needs?

But the more I thought about it ... I didn't want to admit it, but maybe he was right. Already there was a trickle of doubt: I'd seen Oskar that morning, had followed him to the depot. I'd seen him get in the truck and drive down to the border in Lichtenrade. After that, I'd followed his lorry to Ruhleben, then his car to Grunewald—all without a positive sighting of him from the time he left West Berlin to the moment he entered the villa in Grunewald.

At that point I'd been a couple of hundred metres away, watching from behind. I'd had sight of him for less than a second, but I could still be certain it was him: his size, his build, his shock of distinctive grey hair.

But if we were going to split hairs, sure, all I saw in Grunewald was someone matching Oskar's description. Which meant, strictly speaking, I couldn't confirm that person had actually been Oskar. There was a theoretical possibility that it had been someone else.

Pozdniakov, seeing understanding flicker behind my eyes, nodded slowly. "And in the little woodland near Mittenwalde?" he prompted.

My mind obediently followed the Russian major's directions, returning to the day I'd hidden in the woods, waiting for Oskar and his contact. Had that been a brush past, Oskar exchanging a package with the motorcyclist? Or something else?

Was it possible that Oskar had swapped places with the motorcyclist?

The pattern of Oskar's deliveries suddenly made sense. Always two trips, always between one and three days apart, enough time for the motorcyclist to swap places with Oskar, travel to West Berlin for a debriefing, then return, changing places with Oskar again, who'd then bring the truck back to West Berlin.

"And your famously stringent border formalities? Talk me through how, if Oskar had a doppelgänger, he could get through the border checkpoint so easily—just in theory, of course." The Russian was enjoying himself at my expense, but I deserved it. I should have registered this possibility earlier.

"The crossing point in Lichtenrade is dedicated to the waste transports, now and again it's used for construction materials, too. But compared to public crossings the passport and identity checks are relatively lax. Pass and Control Units are mostly concerned with making sure there are no stowaways when the vehicles go back to West Berlin. On entry to the GDR, drivers are checked, and on leaving, both drivers and vehicles are checked. Oskar times his journeys so that he enters the GDR and is checked by one shift, but leaves after shift change, so the driver is checked by another team on the return journey. As long as Oskar and the second person match physically and make sure that each team only ever sees one of the Oskars then there should be no difficulties. But that's a big if. It's practically out of the question that both individuals would be similar enough to the picture in the passport—and they'd both have to use the same passport because the control unit has a copy to double check."

I thought about it some more. Possible, but unlikely. Then another thought struck me: "I'd like to compare the shift records-"

"Rolling shift," interrupted Pozdniakov. "Oskar and his friend always make the second journey after the shift plan has changed. Oskar is always seen by the first platoon, his friend only ever by the second."

"If you know all this, why haven't you stopped him?"

"Oskar is serving peace," answered Pozdniakov, using the generally accepted code for being on a secret mission in the operational area.

That started off a new train of thought: I'd seen Oskar as a West Berlin citizen, clearly involved in activities designed to damage the GDR. But now a KGB officer was telling me he was on our side.

Pozdniakov read the confusion on my face, but far from explaining, he just changed the subject: "Operation RYaN—not your department and in any case above your security level—RYaN monitors and responds to the threat of imperial pre-emptive nuclear missile attacks. Reagan is continuing his sabre-rattling, first the Pershing missiles in West Germany, then Star Wars. Since last month, when the Korean Airlines flight was shot down over Soviet airspace, RYaN has been running hot."

I'd watched the reports about the civil airplane on Western television. The Americans were claiming it had suffered navigation difficulties, causing it to veer over Kamchatka and Sakhalin. Soon after, it had crashed into the sea. The Soviet Union denied all knowledge of what might had happened to the plane and the West were claiming the plane had been fired upon—something the KGB major was now confirming.

"A few weeks later," Pozdniakov continued, "a systems malfunction in the OKO system showed Intercontinental Ballistic Missiles heading towards the Soviet Union. It was a false alarm, but at the time it was taken seriously. It could have been the end of all of us.

"Finally, over the last couple of weeks we've been receiving reports of a large-scale military mobilisation in western Europe. NATO says it's just an exercise. The General Secretary of the CPSU asks what better way to disguise preparations for war?"

I was leaning back now, holding my hands up in front of me, as if to shield myself from what the Russian was saying. Technical malfunctions, civilian airliners being shot down, narrowly averted nuclear apocalypse, the judgement of General Secretary Andropov being questioned ...

As Pozdniakov had already said, too dangerous to believe.

But the Russian hadn't finished yet: "The First Main

Directorate of the KGB has appointed a technical officer to liaise with the Western Allies. It's an unofficial gesture of goodwill, an attempt to avert nuclear war. The liaison is the person you saw in Grunewald."

"And Oskar?"

"Oskar is nothing but a lorry driver, chosen for his surprising resemblance to our technical officer."

I wanted a drink, but a cigarette would have to do. The hand holding the match shook as I struck it.

What was this crazy Russian telling me? Crazy or not, he was right that nobody would believe me if I ever reported what I'd heard.

I smoked the butt, then chained another one off the embers. The KGB officer wandered around a bit more, examining mounds of rubble and broken walls.

When the second cigarette was burnt out, I decided it was time to pull myself together. I'd wanted to see Pozdniakov because I needed something from him and now was the time to ask for it.

"I need logistical support in the case of Major Blecher-" I began, but the Russian cut me off. I saw his hand rise in an impatient gesture as he strode closer to where I was standing.

"The agreement was that you deal with your little problem yourself." I noticed that *our* problem had become exclusively mine. That didn't bode well.

He pulled his own deck of cigarettes out and lit one. Same kind as that night in West Berlin: stubby brown things, the smell of the smoke acrid.

"Your plan, is it clean?" he asked. "Will there be any comeback?"

"There'll be no way to tie it to me—provided I get the logistical support I mentioned."

The KGB major didn't respond. He smoked his cigarette until it must have been burning his fingers, then stepped on it. He picked the butt off the floor and put it in his pocket.

"Tell me then. What is it you need?" when he finally spoke, his voice was cold.

"I need to go to West Berlin, but without leaving a record of the crossing."

Pozdniakov didn't ask why I couldn't organise that myself, he just raised his chin. I wasn't sure whether he was agreeing that it was possible or merely indicating that he'd heard my request.

"The other thing I need," I told him, "is an AKM rifle." Pozdniakov chuckled as he turned away. He was striding towards the door now, it looked like that was all the answer I was going to get.

He opened the door before turning back to me. His silhouette was clear against the lights outside. His face was mostly in shadow, but I could swear I saw his mouth turned up in that ugly half smile of his.

"When do you need all of this?" he asked.

"This afternoon. Early evening at the latest."

The Russian walked out into the yard.

The last thing I heard as the door slotted into its frame:

"I'll be in touch."

71
WEST BERLIN
Spandau

I was in position by 2340, in good time to observe shift change on the border and to keep an eye out for any unusual movements. Behind the Wall, the security strip was lit up like the Friedrichstadtpalast, which left the forest on both sides of the border in deepest shadow.

Rain filtered through the trees, threading over the oilskin I had wrapped around myself and seeping into the sand and pine needles around me. Another piece of oilskin cloth by my side covered the machine pistol KM-72, the Kalashnikov model the Russians term an AKM, and which the lower ranks in the NVA and Border Troops of the GDR affectionately call their *Kaschi*.

The border guards' relief arrived at ten past midnight, two figures trudging along the patrol road, coming from the east. A short exchange of greetings and reports and the old shift began their walk back to base, *Kaschis* slung around their bodies to stay dry under the capes.

The two relief guards waited until the old shift was out of sight, then went behind the watchtower. A scrape of metal against concrete told me they'd opened the door and were going inside, into the dry and warmth.

I focussed my binoculars on the windows at the top of the round tower, but the floodlights were reflecting in the glass, making it impossible to see inside. I shifted around under my oilskin, trying to get comfortable—still more than two and a half hours to wait.

I scanned the visible sector of the border, sweeping from left to right and back again, using the binoculars every so often for a change. This is how a shift as a border guard must feel. Cold, wet, nervous yet bored. Just waiting for something to happen, but hoping nothing will.

I had plenty of time to think, plenty of time to consider what had brought me to these woods on the wrong side of the border.

One of Pozdniakov's men had picked me up a few hours ago. The meeting place had been in a derelict factory in Hohenschönhausen, not far from the prison where this sorry story began. A light grey Ford, diplomatic plates, had driven in and the driver had opened the boot without saying a word or even looking directly at me.

An hour later the boot opened and I was helped out. I stretched my arms and walked around a bit to get the circulation going again, all the time trying to work out where I'd landed.

We were on a sandy track, trees around us. No lights other than the car's to be seen anywhere. Just the regular swishing of a motorway from somewhere behind us. When I turned around, the silent driver was getting back in the car. He shut the door and drove off.

Within a minute or two I made out another pair of headlights heading down the track towards me. I moved out of sight, just behind the first row of trees, and watched as the car came to a halt. An Audi, light colour paintwork, but in the pale moonlight it was impossible to say exactly what colour it might have been. The driver wound down his window and looked into the woods, trying to find me. I stepped forward and he gestured impatiently.

"*Sadis' nazad.*" He jerked his head backwards, indicating the back door of the car. I slid onto the back seat, a long canvas bag was waiting for me, a quick grope told me there was a rifle and two magazines inside.

"Where to," he asked, still speaking in Russian.

"Spandau forest, drop me off near the Johannisstift."

The driver put the car into gear without answering. At some point we hit the Avus motorway, clearly identifiable by its length and lack of curves, then we headed first north then west, into Spandau.

The streets were empty at this time of night, light from the apartments on either side of the road leaked into the night.

The apartments gave way to tidy terraces, then individual houses in their own gardens. Finally we rattled over the tracks of the goods railway and passed the gates of the Johannisstift. A few hundred metres further on I checked the back window: no following headlights, we were on our own.

I told the driver to pull in and I got out, taking the long canvas bag with me.

0250 hours was Time X, when Blecher was scheduled to signal me from the other side of the border. In order to get that far he needed to pass at least two checkpoints and with all probability have to answer to vigilant policemen further back in the hinterland of the border.

I had no doubt that he would be able to bluff his way through, but his passage would be logged and reported upwards.

That didn't bother me.

If things went according to plan then the fact that his movements had been noted would actually help. Nor was there much immediate risk for the major: at this time of night they wouldn't be able to get hold of anyone in the Ministry with the necessary authority to order the detention of a Stasi major.

My biggest worry was that he'd blunder into a tripwire and be detained by border guards. If that happened, it would be much harder for him to talk his way out.

I was spending too much time thinking about Blecher, calculating and recalculating the chances he'd turn up on time. My biggest concern should be that I had no backup plan if things went wrong. If the major was prevented from getting as far as the border defences then I'd have to come up with something else before he—or Pozdniakov—ran out of patience with me.

Pozdniakov wanted Blecher out of the way, Blecher was interfering in his operation. I didn't have any sympathy for the Stasi officer: he was vain and incompetent, didn't deserve his position in a Chekist organisation. But whenever my thoughts took me that far, I'd see the little girl on the bike, the wife at the window.

I shouldn't allow my mind to wander, I had to concentrate. I breathed out slowly, trained the binoculars on the watchtower and counted the joints in the pre-cast concrete rings.

Anything to get my mind away from Blecher and his family.

72
WEST BERLIN
Spandau

As Time X approached, I found it easier to focus on the job at hand, mentally noting all activity, assessing whether it was out of the ordinary.

A *Stoffhund* had driven by an hour ago.

One of the guards from the tower had gone into the shadows just over half an hour ago. He'd left his *Kaschi* behind and returned a minute or two later: call of nature.

By 0247 my focus was completely on the forest on the other side of the brightly lit border. If Blecher failed to turn up, or if one of the border guards appeared at just the wrong moment then my plan would fail.

I was using the binoculars to scan the fringes of the forest when the sound of an engine alerted me to the approach of a vehicle. It wasn't the two-stroke skirl of the *Stoffhund*, it was a steady four-beat, coming from this side of the Wall.

I caught sight of the approaching jeep—it stayed in the shadow of the Wall, making it difficult from this distance to tell whether it was a Land Rover or an Iltis that was skidding through the soft sand along the border. The engine pitch rose as they reached the start of the slope, then the gears changed down and the jeep idled to a stop in the middle of the track.

Two soldiers got out, I couldn't see them clearly, but their silhouettes matched what I could expect: combat trousers tucked into boots, baggy smock cinched with a wide belt and military police caps.

They didn't bother closing the car doors, but headed up the hill—directly towards me. I loosened the oilskin and began to crawl back, hoping the beating rain would snuff out any sound made by the rustling fabric. The two Brits knew the way, they confidently strode up the hill.

By the time they were half-way up the slope, I'd rolled to the side, taking cover behind a double-trunked pine that forked at hip height. The soldiers reached the place I'd been lying and turned around, training their binoculars along the border with the GDR.

One was taller and leaner than the other, who was clearly less fit, breathing heavily after the short climb. While the short MP soon dropped his field glasses and concentrated his gaze in the direction of the vehicle, the tall one continued scanning the security strip. Over his shoulder, I could see the watchtower, from inside a glint of reflected light told me my colleagues in the Border Troops were wide awake and using their own binoculars to observe the class enemy.

Words were exchanged in English and the tall one started back down the hill. Shorty headed straight towards me. He looked around, much more intensely than when he'd been observing the border. His eyes scanned the shadows beneath the trees.

Slowly, I reached down and drew a combat knife, bringing it up to shoulder height while at the same time easing my knees further forwards so I was prepared to jump up.

The British MP was just the other side of the forked pine, I could see the angle of his head and cap—his eyes were focussed on the air above me. With a shrug of his shoulder, he brought his rifle around to the front of his body, his shoulder tilting again as he reached down. I couldn't move any further without disturbing the cape that was still wrapped around my back, but unless I freed myself from the oilcloth, I wouldn't be able to spring up if the *Engländer* brought his gun to bear.

My thighs were tensed, my elbows firm against the earth below, the knife held before me in my right fist.

Just as my left palm met the ground to give me the balance I needed to rush him, I was distracted by a trickling noise. It came from the other side of the pine trunk. A splashing and dripping as the soldier pissed, less than fifty centimetres away from my head.

I didn't leap up, but I couldn't relax either, not until he'd done up his flies and stumbled back down the slope to join his colleague.

I remained alert and ready until I heard the engine growl then diminish as they continued their patrol. As soon as I could see their red tail-lights I checked my watch: 0303.

I'd missed Blecher's first signal, the second and final chance was in two minutes.

I shrugged off the cape and pulled the Kalashnikov out of its oilcloth, then moved forward so I had a good view of the forest opposite. My hand went to my thigh pocket, reaching for the torch. The rain was still falling, my field cap was soaked through and moisture was gathering on my forehead, trickling through my eyebrows. I wiped my eyes, still scanning the edge of the woods, and there—two short flashes, about fifty metres to my right.

I took my torch out, pointed it to the right of where I'd seen Blecher's signal, making it harder to spot from the watchtower, then thumbed the switch. One. Two. Three.

Immediately dropping the torch and grabbing the *Kaschi*, I ran sixty paces to my right, staying parallel with the Wall. I dropped to one knee, the rifle stock pressed to my shoulder, aiming the sights at one of the steel plates that cover the loopholes in the concrete structure of the watchtower. Range: slightly over a hundred metres.

I waited for Blecher to show himself.

There he was, wearing dark clothes, a dark knitted cap, running towards the border, torso doubled over pumping legs.

He fell to his knees in front of the fence, pushed the ring spanner over the counter nut and starting to unwind it. He put the second spanner on the next nut and undid that before moving on to the next bolt.

I'd seen no reaction from the watchtower, if they'd noticed my signal then they were still looking where I'd been and not where I was now.

Blecher had undone one edge of the fencing panel and was shuffling over to undo the other side, throwing anxious glances in the direction of the watchtower.

"Come on you pen-pusher, you can do it, just a couple of bolts," I whispered encouragement to my superior officer, encouragement he'd never hear.

The last nut was free and Blecher was pulling on work gloves, the better to handle the sharp edges of the fence panel. He worked slowly, carefully laying the grille in the soft sand like I'd told him to. Now he was down on his hands and knees, already half-way through the hole he'd made, one metre into the floodlit strip, then two.

That was my cue. With a final squint down the notch and bead of the rifle, I squeezed off a single shot at the loophole in the watchtower. The sharp crack of the shot, a spark as the bullet glanced off the steel.

I didn't wait to see how the border guards would react, I pulled back a pace or two, so that the tower was hidden behind a tree then swung the muzzle of the Kalashnikov around to Blecher. He had already turned, was running back to the hole in the first fence.

Perfect.

As he knelt down to crawl through the gap I breathed out, lined up the sights and squeezed again. A double tap this time, two bullets whizzing towards my superior officer. His back arched and his arms went out, fingers splayed.

He was already dead by the time the guards in the tower started shooting.

73
WEST BERLIN
Spandau

I wrapped the rifle in the oilcloth, picked up the torch and my cape, then used a fallen branch to brush away any signs that I'd been here. The Alarm Group would be arriving soon on the other side, looking for further border violators. Their attentions would be focussed purely over there, but the British military police would probably have heard the shooting and would be back to investigate.

I needed to get some distance in before they started nosing around.

I made the rendezvous with Pozdniakov's driver and lay on the back seat as he took me back to the Grunewald forest. When I got out of the back of the car, Pozdniakov himself was waiting for me. He nodded and turned away, walking twenty, thirty steps. Far enough that the driver couldn't overhear.

"Well?" he asked in German.

"A successful mission. Major Blecher will no longer interfere in your affairs," I reported, also in German. "They'll be scratching their heads over why he tried to leave the GDR this way, but in the end the investigation will conclude that he met his death during a failed attempt to reach the West."

Pozdniakov nodded. He fished a packet of cigarettes out of the breast pocket of his tunic and doled one out for each of us, holding a match up to light first mine then his own. I breathed in the harsh tobacco smoke, my first cigarette since a lifetime ago. It felt good, it felt like the first cigarette on a Sunday morning.

"Tell me."

"The border guards thought they were being shot at and returned fire. Bullets will have been lost in the sand, they won't notice a couple extra. The Kalashnikov is in the car." I held the cigarette in the cup of my hand, protecting it from the rain. There wasn't much of it left.

"You're sure there's no connection between you both?"

"Major Blecher was very discreet about our meetings. The Scout that took me into West Berlin doesn't know who I am. My own superior officer isn't aware of Blecher's involvement."

For a moment the only sound was the hissing of the rain, the only movement that of the glowing cigarettes.

"The motorbike used by Oskar and his double—it had civilian plates, registered to a Border Regiment ..." I left the question hanging.

"There always has to be a red herring," the Russian answered. He ground his cigarette out on the sole of a boot then put the butt in his jacket pocket.

We both turned as a second car came down the trail. It was the Ford with the diplomatic plates. The driver got out and opened up the boot. Pozdniakov held a hand out.

I shook it.

It was dawn before I reached my flat. I stripped off my clothes, dumping them in the corner of the bathroom before climbing under the shower. I turned it up hot, as hot as I could bear. Then I turned it up some more.

I stood there, hands against the wall, head down, watching the sand and pine needles spiralling the plughole. The scalding water drummed, riddling my back.

When I closed my eyes I could still see Major Blecher sagging into the sand as the bullets entered his body.

Second Lieutenant Reim
will return in **Berlin Centre**